BORN GROWN

The Making of Travis C. Burrell

BORN GROWN

The Making of Travis C. Burrell

Jo Evans Lynn

&

Travis C. Burrell

Parchment Global Publishing
1500 Market Street, 12th Floor, East Tower
Philadelphia, Pennsylvania, 19102
www.parchmentglobalpublishing.com

The characterizations in this book are depicted through the eyes of a child 5-13 years old. We have kept the portrayals of people and events as true to his recollections as possible.

ISBN: 978-1-952302-13-8 (hc)
ISBN: 978-1-952302-11-4 (sc)
ISBN: 978-1-952302-12-1 (e)

Library of Congress Control Number: 2020915239

Chapter

1

His family wasn't right. At the age of five, he didn't have the vocabulary to put the not "right" parts into words. Still, he knew that the other kids in his kindergarten class arrived for their first day of school with mothers, fathers, grandmas, or in a couple of cases with an older sibling who introduced them to the teacher.

Travis had come to school alone on the school bus.

He knew which bus to get on because he'd seen some of the kids, he hung out with getting on it.

He wasn't worried about not having a grownup with him. He could and did take care of himself all the time. He was concerned about his little brothers, though. He thought back to the directions that he'd given his middle brother, Anthony, about keeping himself and Rodney safe.

"Anthony, I'm going to school. So, it's up to you to look out for Rodney." Rodney was their baby brother. He was almost a year old with dark brown eyes that were as big as the ones on those babies on jars of Gerber® baby food. Rodney had fair skin like their mother and good hair like their mother claimed to have had before she started putting perms in her hair when she got to high school.

"I know what to do. You told me a zillion times. If Ma goes out and brings home one of those men that like to touch pretty-little-boys like Rodney, I take Rodney to Byron's Mom. If Dad comes home crazy mean or high, I hide both of us until you come to get us." Anthony repeated the directions in a sing-song voice.

He was tired of Travis trying to be the boss of him. He was four and nearly as tall as Travis. Only ten months and two weeks in age separated them. They looked so much alike-lean angular features with huge light brown eyes-that people often mistook them for twins. He'd keep Rodney safe not because Travis told him to do it but because that's what big brothers did.

Travis didn't care about Anthony having an attitude as long as he did what he told him to do.

Yeah, he reassured himself. He'd told Anthony all he needed to know. They would be all right until he got back home.

*   *   *

The first thing Travis noticed on the bus that morning was that all the other kids, even the ones from Turner Courts had on new looking clothes. He felt a bit better when he looked across the aisle at his best friend. Byron's clothes weren't new.

He'd seen Byron wearing the same blue shirt to church last week, but Byron's Mom had washed it and sprayed something called starch on it as she ironed it. She'd even starched and ironed creases in his pants even though Byron begged her not to. Everyone, except Bryon's Mom, knew that men in the projects where they lived in South Dallas, Texas, didn't wear starched and creased jeans.

Although Byron was almost two years older than him, Travis looked out for Byron and kept the older boys and mean girls from picking on him too much. By too much, Travis meant more than the normal amount of getting picked on that every kid who has big ears, nappy hair, Aunt Jemima lips or any other feature that makes them look or act different from the other kids has to put up with. Travis was offended for Byron's sake when he was picked on because of his lazy eye and bright pink lips, but Byron laughed along with his taunters.

Travis also kept the older boys and mean girls from taking Byron's ice-cream and grocery money. It wasn't that Byron was scared to fight. He was such a sweet natured kid that he liked and trusted everyone.

In school, Byron had been labeled "dull average" or a slow learner. Which didn't make sense to Travis because Byron could sing all the words to any song he'd ever heard. Since Byron's Mom listened to all kinds of music from 'oldies but goodies' from the 50s, 60s, and 70's to jazz and gospel, that meant he knew the words to hundreds of songs. How could someone who could do that be a slow learner?

Older boys and mean girls took advantage of Byron's willingness to hand over his ice cream or grocery money to anyone who asked for it. He would start crying when they wouldn't give his ice cream back like Travis always did after taking one lick. When someone took his grocery money, he would hand them the list of groceries expecting them to take his money to the store. He'd wait patiently for hours for them to return.

That's how Travis met Byron. Travis found Byron standing on the corner crying as he waited for some guys who had probably taken his mother's money to the liquor store or the nearest crack house. Travis recognized Bryon as the son of the pleasingly plump woman who always had a smile and good word for everyone. She didn't work. Not because she didn't want to work. She'd worked as a maid for a rich woman since she was a teenager, but her oldest child was born with multiple deformities, with nubs instead of legs and an oddly shaped head. Mazie, that was her name, could not speak but she could hear. Mazie bobbed her head to the beat of music and she had the most endearing smile.

Although the woman for whom Byron's Mom had worked for nearly 10 years agreed to pay for someone to take care of Mazie so that she could continue to work, after Byron's Mom found bruises on Mazie where she had been pinched or handled roughly, she stayed home and cared for her daughter.

It meant accepting Welfare and Medicaid. These had been lowering circumstances for a woman who had lied about her age to get work to help her mother take care of her younger siblings when she was a full year too young to get a worker's permit. The words, "A mother does what she has to do to take care of her children," seemed to be her motto.

That long-ago day when Travis had found Byron crying, Byron's Mom thanked Travis, for bringing her son home, with one of her famous little sweet potato pies. That was it. The bond between the two boys was set. Travis the protector and Byron the protected.

*   *   *

Byron looked clean and neat in his blue shirt and starched and creased pants. Travis pulled the yellow and green stripped t-shirt and pants he was wearing from a pile of dirty clothes in the corner of the room that he shared with his two brothers. The clothes weren't clean but at least they didn't smell too much like pee.

Yesterday, Byron's mother had insisted on washing Travis' face and hands after the two boys finished the ice cream, she bought them from the ice-cream truck. So, he knew the parts that people could see were mostly clean.

He did not feel sorry for himself because the other children had new clothes or at least clothes that were clean. Self-pity wasn't in his nature. Instead, what was growing in him even at the age of five was a determination to do better to get things right.

Travis was already what could be called a Watcher. People always noticed his eyes because they were two shades lighter than his milk chocolate complexion. His eyes were constantly darting from place to place- checking out everything.

Especially the adults. Other kids might have to worry about bullies their own age, but there was an air of toughness about Travis that made boys twice his size and age leave him alone. In his world, adults were the more present source of fear and pain.

He watched the adults and the world around him like a seasoned detective-taking in things that kids who didn't have to worry about getting slapped upside the head for the least infraction never noticed.

He watched grownup's eyes.

He knew that eyes clouded with drugs were unpredictable. A kid with good sense got as far away as he could get from drugged-up eyes. Travis had good sense and he made sure that he hid his two little brothers away with him. At four and 10 months old, his little brothers understood that there was safety in being quiet.

Crying wasn't a tool in their arsenal. Finding a safe place under a bed or under a pile of dirty clothes and keeping their mouths shut until the danger passed-made more sense to them.

So, Travis had learned early to watch quietly. His habit of watching either made the people around him nervous or convinced them that he was smart.

Travis watched the teacher interact with the parents and the other students in his class.

She wasn't very tall, and her mixed gray hair was pulled back from her face with an animal print hairband. Travis would later learn that the hairbands that matched her dress, earrings, and shoes were kind of like her trademark. Although the grey hair documented the more than twenty-five years she'd been teaching, her dark brown complexion was free of wrinkles and the frown lines that Travis associated with mean adults.

After watching the teacher, a while, he went up to her and introduced himself, "I'm Mr. Travis Burrell."

"Mister?" she fought to contain her smile. She'd worked with inner-city boys like him long enough to know that laughing at anything he said was the kiss of death to any teacher-student relationship. There were no second chances with boys like him. Once they decided that you were one of "those people- people who'd decided that boys like him weren't worth their time- boys like this one never let you back in.

"I'm Miss Echols. Is it all right that I call you Travis?"

He looked at her with serious eyes like the eyes of a seventy-year-old man and said, "You don't know me like that Ma'am."

It was the politeness of the Ma'am and the conviction in his eyes that convinced her to call him Mister Travis for the rest of the school year.

*   *   *

Mister Travis discovered that kindergarten wasn't so bad. He'd never been in daycare or had parents who were willing to spend time preparing him for school by reading to him and teaching him the alphabet and such. The teacher started out calling him a "Blank Slate" and ended the year calling him a "Sponge".

His mother had graduated from college, but both his parents got caught-up in in the drug culture of the eighties. His Dad mostly dealing and his Mom using.

Lucky for Travis, he inherited the brains of a class valedictorian, the agility and physical grace of a natural athlete and the polite charm of a seasoned diplomate.

He watched the kids who came from the "right" homes and mimicked their behavior and soon passed most of them socially and academically.

It seemed that he already knew somethings that he didn't even know that he knew-like traffic signs, colors, shapes, and life words like STOP, DON'T WALK, EXIT and DANGER.

Chapter
2

Miss Echols believed in celebrating every little success with a gold star and lavish compliments and everyone's birthday by making the day special for the birthday boy or girl. The class Mom's took turns supplying the cupcakes and a tiny cake with candles for the birthday boy or girl. Miss Echols supplied a small personalized wrapped gift for each child.

Travis really wasn't expecting anything. Birthdays were just another day to get through. His mother hadn't signed up to do anything. But on his birthday, he got a cake with six candles to blowout and a writing tablet with his name, Mr. Travis C. Burrell, engraved on it.

Mister Travis held that writing tablet close to his chest the rest of the day and pushed the slice of cake that the teacher had wrapped in foil for him to take home deeper into his pocket more times than he could count.

When it was time to go home, Mister Travis followed the rest the class out of the classroom, but he slipped into the bathroom rather than getting on bus 436, the bus that usually took him and 41 other students to their end of Turner Courts.

When he was sure that the bus had gone, he went back to his classroom.

"What happened? Did you miss your bus?" Miss Echols was surprised that he was still there. The process for delivering each child to the correct bus or to the car riders waiting area had been fine-tuned by the middle of the school year to the point that nothing unexpected ever happened.

"No Ma'am. I didn't miss it. I know how to get to my house, but I wanted to tell you something first," he swallowed hard as though the words were stuck in his throat. He'd said, "Thank you" like the other boy in his class who happened to have the same birthday. Travis knew now that saying "Thank you" was good manners but the words really hadn't meant much to him until today.

"I wanted to tell you that it's all right for you to call me Travis."

She almost told him that she could have called him Travis all along. After all, she was the teacher and the adult authority figure in the classroom. She didn't say it though because she understood that boys like Travis needed to hold on to whatever little bit of self-respect that labels like *Mister* and *Young Man* offered them.

So, she'd let him hold on to the bravado and the air of toughness that helped boys like him get through somethings that some grown men could not withstand.

She said, "I appreciate that Travis. Tell you what, give me a few minutes and I'll drive you home."

"You don't have to do that Ma'am. I know the way," Travis insisted while turning to leave on his own. He heard her call his name but kept running.

He didn't want her to see where he lived. It wasn't that it was the worst place he'd lived. Before they got into Turner Courts his family bounced around from place to place. Although his parents had three sons together, it hadn't been until after Rodney was born that their father came to live with them fulltime. When he wasn't there, the rent didn't get paid even when he gave the money to their Mom. So, they'd get put out of wherever they were living every two or three months. No, he wasn't ashamed of Turner Courts, but he knew what people who didn't live there said about it and them.

Even though most of the women in Turner Courts worked one or two jobs, Other People said that the women who lived in Turner Courts were all Welfare Moms. Other People said that they were women who popped out babies every year to keep their Welfare checks coming. Other People called them lazy whores who sat on their behinds all day watching soap operas and letting their children run wild.

If they said terrible things about their mothers, they had even lower opinions of the children those women produced. Other People said that their male children were slow-witted, lazy discipline problems, and the girls were fast. The boys, no matter how bright they seemed outside the classroom almost without fail, ended up in Special Education classes. The girls almost without fail, whether they went to church regularly or not, ended up pregnant in their teens.

Projects were never intended to be unsavory places to live. After World War II, much of the African American population migrated from rural areas to cities such as Dallas. All of these poor people moving into the city compounded housing problems. The city's method of solving this problem was the building of five housing projects.

Ma Turner had told Travis that Turner Courts was named for one of her husband's relatives. His name was J.L. Turner Sr., one of the first black attorneys in the state of Texas. The early residents saw Turner Courts as a place that had been built as a tribute to all the men who served their country during World War II. When the 294 Units were first built, the people took pride in the little plot of land outside their apartment buildings. Many planted flowers and an occasional tomato vine and some cooking herbs.

Those early occupants thought of the projects as a starting place until they could afford to buy their own homes and move to Bonton, the wealthier section of South Dallas. There were still some people like that in Turner Courts during the mid-eighties. But now many were like Travis' parents so bogged down in the drug culture that they had no interest in their homes. Their plots. Themselves or their children.

No, he didn't want her to see where he lived, but even more than that, he didn't want Miss Echols to meet his Mom or see the roaches that didn't have the common decency to wait until night-time to come out. When he got home from school, the cockroaches would be sitting on the coffee table with their legs crossed, eating the crumbs leftover from last night's dinner.

It was the first and last birthday cake and present that Mr. Travis would receive until his tenth birthday.

*   *   *

Although he got along with most of his classmates, Travis didn't make friends in kindergarten. One friend was enough for him. Because of his relationship with Byron, he saw friends as a responsibility. His brothers and Byron were more than enough for a five -year old to handle. Besides, the kids in his class who lived in Bonton, where wealthier African Americans lived were warned by their parents to stay away from boys and girls from Turner Courts.

Whenever Travis or one of his other classmates from Turner Courts tried to join a game, the other children would get quiet, and seconds later, the game would be over. The children would move away and form another game as far away as they could get turning their backs to the would-be intruders.

It wasn't overt meanness or bullying, but it hurt anyway.

*   *   *

Travis' favorite subject was math. It was the only subject he felt he'd have any real use for in life. His dad was forever cussing about someone cheating him or cutting him "short."

He told Travis, "Learn to count your money boy. Folks will cheat you when they think, you're too high or too stupid to know you've been cheated."

Travis had no intention of ever getting high. He knew too much about what getting high did to his mother and father. His father liked the money from selling drugs too much to get or keep a regular job and his mother stayed too high to get out of bed before 1:00p.m.

Worse than that, both parents were mean when they came down off a high. Their father would fight with words that incited their mother to throw things and attempt to scratch his eyes out. They'd fight each other all night long or until one of them got their hands on enough money to get high again.

He had no intention of getting high, but he knew that knowing how to count his money was important to living "right."

Chapter

3

Not right got much worse. At the beginning of first grade, his father stopped coming home. September 13, 1987 was burned into Travis' memory. Years later, when his ninth-grade teacher asked her students to write an epiphany story about the single event that marked the end of their childhood, Travis would write about "The Time When My Dad Stopped Coming Home."

His Dad was a good-looking man. Everybody said so. He wore his naturally curly hair cut short, but even with pomade slicking it down the natural waves could be seen. Travis and Rodney had inherited his light brown eyes, but the laugh lines around his eyes made him seem more approachable at 32 than either of his sons. His Dad had a dimple in his chin that Travis often heard his mother say made her want to, "Drop her drawers the first time she saw him." Travis didn't know what drawers were, but he figured they were something nasty the way his parents hugged and kissed every time she said that.

It wasn't unusual for his Dad to spend a few days with one of his other women, but he usually turned up again after two or three days at the most. His mother still looked pretty good back then, so she wasn't worried about any other woman taking him away from her.

She said, "He's a dog and he do what dogs do-go stiffing around for some tail. He'll be back. When he gets back here, I'm gonna give him a piece of my mind that will burn his ears off."

As much as Travis and his brothers wanted their Dad to come back, they dreaded the hours of arguing and shouting that usually went along with their Dad's return. Their Mom would scream like a banshee. She cussed enough to take the bark off a tree and throw anything at him that she could pick up. By 1987, there wasn't anything in the house that wasn't broken or glued or taped back together.

Whenever he came back from being away for a while their dad never cussed or hit her. After he'd had enough, he figured she was entitled to some cussing and fussing, he'd grab her from behind, hold her close, and whisper in her ear until she calmed down. He'd pick her up and carry her into the bedroom. Then everything would be back to not quite right until the next time...

*   *   *

The first weekend that his Dad didn't come back home wasn't so bad because they all believed that he'd walk in the door at his usual time on Monday. Then they were pretty sure that he would be back by Tuesday and if not that day then the next day for certain. He'd always come back before.

At first, their Mom kept up her usual routine. She got up around 1:00p.m. Washed up, got dressed, took her rollers out of her hair, and put on her make-up. It never ceased to amaze Travis how she would put rollers in her hair no matter how late she got in bed or how torn up she was from liquor or drugs. She spent more time putting on her makeup than anything else.

In her mind she was still Lisa Gregory the homecoming queen and head cheerleader- the darling of all who knew her. The deaths of both her parents before she was nine years old would have been a sob story for any other girl, but it wasn't for her because her big brother, John Gregory, was a local football star. The fact that he had also been a good student elevated the status of his siblings at school and in the community. All the other girls wanted to look like her and dress like her. All the guys wanted to be with her.

A hurtful thought went through her mind when she thought about her "Glory days."

She'd been so afraid of losing it all-the popularity and having the Nobody Girls being jealous of her. It seemed all that would change back during her junior year in high school when she got pregnant, but it hadn't because her boyfriend was a senior.

Everyone blamed him for corrupting such a sweet innocent young thing. She laughed every time she thought about the word *innocent* and even more when she thought about the word *sweet*.

She hadn't been either one of those since she was twelve, when her grandfather's best friend started raping her.

Yeah, she'd been the one who taught her Church Boy boyfriend how to please a woman. The smile always left her eyes when she remembered the look on his face when she refused to marry him and let him make things right.

The fool had said that he loved her.

He hadn't known the truth about love. She did. Love was a myth told by men who only wanted to get under a girl's skirt.

That word *love* came out of the mouths' of men like saliva out of the mouth of a rabid dog.

Lust had nothing to do with love. It was about the way a woman looked.

So, every day she put on enough makeup to change her complexion from a sickly yellow to a pale golden brown and carefully drew on eyebrows that were regularly shaved off with her husband's razor. After she'd checked herself from every angle of the mirror on the old dresser that she'd paid a couple of the older guys to drag in from the curb, she made what she called dinner.

Travis knew that his Mom wasn't much of a cook because he watched Byron's Mom cook real meals from scratch. Fat brown biscuits that looked as fluffy as clouds in the middle accompanied every meal. Byron's Mom used stuff called seasoning and butter to make her food taste good.

She'd do something called sautéing onions before adding them to meat. The smell never failed to make Travis' mouth water.

Travis' Mom opened a box of Kraft Mac & Cheese©, opened a can of Store Brand peas or green beans, and fried a few slices of Spam. Any bread came from a loaf of thin sliced Wonder Bread©.

All of them ate whatever she fixed without complaint.

It was better than nothing.

Nothing was what they got on the seventh day that their Dad didn't come home. *Not right* didn't look so bad now. The good thing about his father coming home was that although he didn't always keep a regular job, he always had a hustle- making just enough for Travis' mother to get her hair done, to pay the rent, keep the water and lights on and to buy a little food.

Their mother was totally dependent on him and too proud to go down to the Social Services office. His mother made it clear to anyone who asked and even to people who didn't care either way that being married to a Burrell didn't change the fact that she was a Gregory to the bone. Gregory's didn't get on Welfare. She was a college graduate. She'd come to Dallas, Texas with big plans. She still had big plans.

In her mind, it was having those boys so close together that had cost her the big-time job at one of the largest oil companies in the world. The fact that she'd been fired before her second son was born for smoking pot on the job had been casually deleted from her catalog of facts. Firing someone for smoking pot on the job was a vailed attempt to keep a Sister from reaching the top of the heap. Hell, she'd needed that pot. Just a couple of puffs before the biggest meeting of her career. The fact that she'd been in the bathroom smoking for close to an hour and turned up nearly half an hour late for the meeting shouldn't have mattered. She was Lisa Gregory. She could do whatever she damn well pleased.

She told the boys that sixth evening after their father stopped coming home, "I'll be damned if I'll go stand in line with a bunch of women in run-over shoes and their tiddies hanging down to the knees. I'm better than that. Gregory's are better than that."

Then for dinner, she served them each a slice of bread soaked in grease and fried.

Travis couldn't help thinking that the Burrell part of him was mighty hungry. He didn't say anything though. He knew if he refused to eat the fried bread his younger brothers would follow his lead.

He noticed that his mother didn't eat any of the greasy bread though. This wasn't unusual. She never ate much because she was always watching her shape. The main grudge she held against each of her sons was that for nine long hard months each of them had messed up her shape.

At the beginning of the second week, Travis' mother didn't get out of bed until late at night for two days. The first day, at around 10:30p.m. she got up. Got dressed, put on her make-up, and went out. She came back a couple of hours later high as the Bank of America Plaza, the tallest building in Dallas in 1987.

The second day, she got dressed, put on her makeup, and hit the streets at about 11:00p.m. When she came back, she brought a man with her and they went straight into the bedroom. When the man left about an hour later Travis peaked into the room and saw that his Mom was either passed-out or asleep. He saw two twenties on the nightstand.

He tip-toed into the bedroom. He said in a whisper,

"Mom, I'm going to the store to get some food. Is it all right if I get a twenty?" She didn't say anything.

Travis hunched his shoulder dismissing any feelings of guilt. He took a twenty-dollar bill off the nightstand. He knew what the forty dollars was for. Every Wednesday evening, no matter how tight money was, his father gave his Mom $40 to get her hair done. It was Wednesday and she'd gotten the money for herself. Travis went to the 7-eleven Store up the street from his apartment building.

"I need some stuff that doesn't need to be in the fridge," Travis told Ma Turner.

It was strange for an older woman like her to take a late-night shift in the Hood, but her husband had had a stroke a few months back. He was back to working a few hours a day, but he got tired easily. So, his wife took over after dinner until the store closed at 2:00a.m. Every store on the strip had been robbed a dozen times or more except this 7-eleven.

The owners Pa and Ma Turner belonged to all of them. Pa Turner was a former football and baseball player at Grambling University. He never claimed to have been a star in either sport, but he said he had what mattered most- Double love for the sport and for competition. He sponsored and helped coach a little league baseball team and all age levels of the Pop Warner Football teams.

Ma Turner was one of those classic African American beauties. She was a little darker than Lena Horn, but her complexion was as faultless. The only clues that she was well into her sixties were the middle age belly and snow-white hair. Height wise, she was tiny-less than five feet tall, but her voice was rich and smokey like a jazz singer. She'd been her husband's college sweetheart.

Although she hadn't worked as a registered nurse for more than 15 years, many of the older residents still called her Nurse Turner. She was never too busy to take care of any hurt no matter how minor.

Every would-be robber knew that his own mama would turn him in if he robbed the Turners.

"Your lights been turned off already? Your Dad hasn't been gone that long," She questioned Travis as she started to gather food in a small basket. Most folks didn't know that his Dad had stopped coming home, but Travis wasn't surprised that Ma Turner knew. She knew everything about everyone- not because she gossiped, but because people confided in her things that they wouldn't tell anyone else.

"If I put it where she can find it, she'll sell it," Travis didn't make a habit of lying unless he absolutely had to.

"You're right about that," Ma Turner didn't try to hide her disgust. To her way of seeing things, women like Travis' mother weren't worth a bucket of spit. God had blessed them with the children she'd prayed for every Sunday until she started going through the change. The boy's dad, Sam Burrell, had come in a month ago asking for an advance until his next pay-day because his wife had sold all their groceries to get money to get high.

Travis left the store with eight cans of Vienna Sausages, eight cans of potted meat, two loaves of bread, a box of instant grits, a jar of grape jelly, a jar of peanut butter, a box of Saltine Crackers and directions to put the $17.82 cents in change that he got back in a safe hiding place.

Chapter

4

Travis made the food last as long as he could. There were seven Wieners in each can of Vienna Sausages*. He cut two into several small pieces and mixed them with some grits to feed Rodney. Then, he cut three in half the long way for Anthony's sandwich. He did the same with the last two weenies for his sandwich. He spread the potted meat thinly on one side of both slices of his brothers' sandwiches and spread it even more thinly on one side of his only slice of bread. **Whatever it took to get by.**

He didn't worry about whether or not his Mom had something to eat.

Now, instead of coming in late or near morning she stayed gone two or three days at a time. When she came in, she usually carried a bag of fast food and a drink. Once when Rodney pulled on her skirt begging for MacDonald's, his generic name for all fast food, she pushed him over on his bottom and yelled, "I know Byron's Mom is feeding y'all some of her Welfare food. That hussy wouldn't give me a crumb off her table. She makes me sick. Threatening to turn me in to social service. Trying to tell me what to do. Let her try it and I'll mess everybody up."

The fact that she was hateful enough to do just that - mess a lot of people up- was probably the reason why people left her alone. Left her children alone.

In Turner Courts, people did what they needed to do to get by. Maybe they allowed a daughter and her child to stay in a three-bedroom apartment that was already four people over the eight people limit. Maybe, six and seven-year-old kids were kept home from school to tend to the younger ones while their mother went to work during the day or to a second job during the night. Maybe, mothers looked the other way when their sons brought home a little money that they'd earned as runners for a drug dealer.

The third week after their father stopped coming home, Byron's Mom offered to give Travis some more of her food, but Travis assured her that his Dad had left him enough money to feed himself and his brothers most of the time. Travis told her with a smile, "We have plenty of food most of the time."

He guessed a little bit of that Gregory pride had rubbed off on him. Every offer of charity seemed to rob him of a bit of his self-reliance.

He could count money so he knew that the way Ma Turner made that twenty dollars "pay" for over a month's worth of food was a type of charity, but the way she went along with his insistence on paying her a little something each time he went to the store allowed him to keep his pride intact.

By mid-November, Travis' mother started staying away for weeks at a time, but that wasn't the worst thing that happened that month.

Ma Turner died.

She just keeled over at the store on November 16th. By the time the ambulance got to the store, nearly the whole neighborhood was crowded outside the store. Everyone came running when they heard the sirens from the ambulance. They weren't coming to signify like people usually do when a fight breaks out. They were purely there out of concern for Ma Turner.

The first word that went out about the incident incited some of the crowd by claiming that some fool had tried to rob the store and scared Ma Turner so bad that she dropped dead.

The members of the crowd who'd heard that version of the story, were there to ensure their own brand of justice to the perpetrator. There was a lot of cussing and swearing and folks promising to beat him down like the low life that he was.

The crowd began to calm down as they listened to Mrs. Towns tell her version of what happened. She was an elderly lady who wore big floppy dime store hats and carried a wicked looking cane more for defense than for walking. She claimed that she knew exactly what took place because she was in the store when it happened. She started her story over and over again for each group of new members of the growing crowd.

She would say, "I saw it all and I ain't got no reason to lie…" She needed this qualifying statement because she was known throughout Turner Courts for gossiping and lying on folks.

Mrs. Towns got more dramatic with each retelling grabbing her chest and swooning into the arms of the nearest man, then recovering to finish the story after a couple of the women fanned her face with funeral home fans that elderly ladies seem to pullout from nowhere like street magicians.

The Medics worked on Ma Turner for nearly forty minutes. Every time they started to halt their efforts; Pa Turner would plead with them to try one more time. They tried again and again and again, but they could not revive her. Pa Turner was so torn up over her death that the medics had to call another ambulance to take him to the hospital.

The next week when Travis went to the store to pick up some more groceries, there was a big hand-written sign on the door that said,

STORE CLOSED INDEFINITELY.

"What does that big word **INDEFINITELY** mean?" Travis spelled it out as he pointed to the sign addressing a group of young men standing around on the corner near the store.

"It means it ain't ever going to open again," Ham Bone, the neighborhood pessimist, said.

"No, it doesn't. It means that they don't know when it will reopen, said Inkie the only one of the group that had actually finished high school.

At the time, Travis chose to believe Inkie, but it turned out that Ham Bone was right.

*   *   *

The next bad thing that happened was that Byron moved out of the projects and took his Mom and younger brother and older sister with him.

Over time, Byron's Mom had started baking a few extra biscuits and threatening to throw them out if Travis didn't accept them. The biscuits and the cheese she gave him cut off of a block of surplus cheese made at least two meals a week for Travis and his brothers.

With two of his regular sources of food gone, Travis had to find some way to get food for himself and his brothers. He'd heard some of the neighbors talking about a food bank at one of the churches. The next day when it was his turn to stay home with Rodney, Travis decided to take Rodney to the food bank in the wagon that Byron had given him last Christmas when Byron's church fulfilled an Angel Tree wish for every child in the church.

Byron had wished for a bicycle. The one he got wasn't new, but it was an extra special gift for a kid like Byron. For the first three months after he got it, Byron wouldn't take it out after it rained because he didn't want to get the tires dirty. Even when he started taking it out more, he kept it cleaned and polished like new.

Travis stood in the Food Bank line for over an hour. Rodney started to cry after the first ten minutes. He'd started crying about every little thing lately. Ma Turner told Travis the month before she died that Rodney was "cutting" teeth. She'd given him something to rub on his gums, but all that was gone.

Travis missed Ma Turner. She made so much of what was going on around him make sense.

Rodney was hungry and cold. Dallas didn't have many cold days in November or any other part of the winter, but mornings often started out around 42° which felt cold to children still wearing their summer shorts and t-shirts. Last winter, Byron's Mom gave Rodney a used but well cared for light blue snowsuit that all of her children had outgrown, but no matter how hard he tried, Travis was unable to stuff Rodney into it.

Although Anthony and Travis had lost five pounds or more since their Dad stopped coming home, Rodney still looked like a tubby toddler. Before they left the house, Travis put three t-shirts on Rodney and wrapped a dirty towel around his shoulders, but Rodney wouldn't stay wrapped up. "I'm here to pick up some food for my Grandma. She's too sick to come stand in line," Travis lied to the woman when it was finally his turn. He didn't feel bad about lying because over half of the guys he once hung-out with were being raised by a Grandma. They'd usually been left by a teenage mother so that she could either go to school or get with someone who didn't want to raise another man's child.

"I'm here to pick up food for my Grandma. She's too sick to come and stand in line," Travis lied looking the woman straight in the eye.

"Well, I'm sorry to hear that, you usually have to be eighteen or older to pick up food, but I'll make an exception for you this one time, but your mother or father will have to come the next time." The tall thin church lady instructed one of the men helping load boxes to put a box in Travis' wagon.

She knew the boy was lying, but there was no way she could deny him food. He was standing so straight, trying to make himself look taller and older, but the narrow shoulders and small boney face clearly told the mother of six boys the story of a very young boy of no more than seven years who had been hungry for a very long time. If he came back next week, she'd probably give him another box of food. She didn't tell him that.

She looked at the cute little boy in the wagon. "Why don't you and that baby have on jackets?" She demanded.

"He's out-grown it," He didn't bother explaining that his denim jacket, that actually belonged to his Dad, had been worn to school that morning by Anthony. They had to take turns wearing Travis' jacket because Anthony had taken his off and put it down on the playground and while he played the jacket had gone missing. They'd watched for another kid wearing Anthony's jacket for over a week, but people moved in and out of Turner Courts so often that they finally gave up.

"It's your blessed day. We've just finished collecting winter coats and jackets for the homeless. Go inside and follow the signs to the Fellowship Hall. Tell them Sister Velma sent you. Get one for yourself and the baby.

Travis almost told her that they weren't homeless. Yet. Their father didn't come home, but he continued to pay the rent, light bill, and such. Once, an envelope with food stamps and a note in it was left in their mailbox next to the door. The note said,

These food stamps should tide you and the boys over until you get yours started. I'll pay the bills until Christmas.

Sam

Travis' mother was so angry when she read the note that she tore it and the food stamps into itsy-bitty pieces.

Travis tried to glue the food stamps back together, but the young lady at the grocery store said it was against the law for her to accept mutilated food stamps. He almost smiled when he thought about those food stamps because he'd learned a big new word that day. MUTILATED- torn up into itsy-bitty pieces.

No, he didn't say that they weren't homeless because Rodney was trembling so hard from the cold that his four new teeth were clicking together like tap shoes.

Travis kept his mouth shut and followed the woman's directions.

The people who were handing out the coats gave Travis a heavy red ski jacket with a black velvet collar and Rodney a fleece coat with a hood and attached mittens. They found a pair of black knitted gloves for Travis. "Could I please have a jacket for my other brother? He had to go to school today wearing my denim jacket and it's not too warm."

"I can't give you three coats. We have more than a dozen needy children already signed up," she huffed at him.

"He's a child, a year younger than me, and he's needing a coat real bad Ma'am," Travis appealed to the Church Lady.

"No. Rules are in place for a reason," she looked down into his serious light brown eyes. Eyes that seemed to preach a sermon about why she and the other volunteers were there.

"I've got to go in back for a minute and nobody had better not give this boy one of those extra coats from that pile over there." She said the last part loud enough to be heard on the other side of Dallas, Texas. Then, she left the room.

"Here, take this one and get away from here before she gets back, an older woman who was barely an inch taller than Travis handed him a navy-blue coat and shooed him away.

As he walked away, Travis looked back over his shoulder and saw the woman who'd said "No" watching him with a smile on her face.

No one could accuse her of breaking the rules.

That night, Travis and his brothers had the closest thing to a real meal that they'd had in a very long time. Travis opened two packs of instant grits, added a cup of hot water from the kitchen sink and cut two slices from the canned ham from the box into itty-bitty pieces and added them to the grits. He opened a can of string beans especially for Rodney. Rodney could eat string beans straight out of the can like other kids could down a box of Cracker Jacks'.

When they'd finished their meal, Travis put the rest of the canned ham in the refrigerator.

Their mother seldom came home anymore. When she did, she continued to take her fast food straight to her room.

She acted as though her children had left home with their Dad.

Chapter
5

Travis realized that there was no magic or math that would make the food in the box last until he could figure out another way to get some more food. It was hard to keep food in the house when it was Anthony's turn to stay home from school with Rodney.

Anthony was always hungry. Whatever Travis or Rodney left on their plate Anthony would finish it off even if he had to lick the plate to do it. When Anthony was in charge, he'd give himself and Rodney second and third helpings. Travis told him time and time again not to do that, but Anthony never listened.

It was as though Anthony just expected Travis to come up with some more food out of thin air. Travis wasn't into five-finger-discounts. Not because he was too honest to steal, but because he'd never had to do it before his Dad stopped coming home.

He knew kids whose mothers would send them to the store with a list and not a dime of money. Those kids hardly ever got caught, but when they did get caught, the time they spent in Juvie wasn't a big loss to their family because most of the families in Turner Courts had seven or more kids. One got caught -send the next one in line.

Travis was all Anthony and Rodney had. He knew if he got caught his brothers would be placed in foster care.

He'd heard horror stories from kids in foster care. The worst stories, to him, were the ones about never seeing your brothers or sisters again. Never being a family again. Even a not right family was better than no family at all.

So, he and Anthony decided to keep the fact that their mother left them alone for weeks at a time a secret from their teachers and other authorities.

Their school had sent a couple of letters about truancy. They'd figured out that the word "truancy" had something to do with them having to take turns staying home with Rodney, because the letters listed the days that each one of them had been absent from school.

The boys decided that since Anthony was just getting started in school and Travis had had perfect attendance the year before that Anthony would go to school the most days unless there was a particular reason why Travis needed to go.

*   *   *

Today just happened to be one of those days. Travis' first grade teacher thought there was something wrong with him because he seemed listless and disinterested in learning. So, she had gotten a school psychologist scheduled to test him for special education.

Travis was determined to show her that he wasn't dumb. He wanted her to know that there was nothing wrong with his head. The only thing that was wrong with him was that most of the time he was weak from hunger and worried about where they were going to get their next meal.

Travis smiled to himself. He wasn't going to be hungry today. He'd found a pack of chewing gum in the left pocket of the coat the Church Lady gave him.

He'd made the gum last over three weeks by methodically breaking off a little piece of a stick of gum and chewing it long pass the point that all the flavor was gone. Then, he'd break off another tiny piece and add it to the flavorless gum. When there was nothing left of that stick of gum, he'd start on the next stick in the pack.

The constant chewing seemed to fool his stomach- at least that's what Travis told himself- that food was on the way. Each night he would store the gum that he'd been chewing on the back of his hand.

By the morning that he was to be tested, he had a wad of gum as big as a plug of chewing tobacco in his mouth.

"Take it out," the psychologist didn't bother with niceties like, "Good morning." Testing this child was a waste of her time. Teachers like Miss Echols got on her last good nerve. They claimed to see potential where there clearly was none. She shook her head thinking about the glowing report from the boy's cumulative folder that Miss Echols had written about his academic performance in kindergarten. She'd written things like – *One of the brightest students I've ever taught. All skills levels well above average. A joy to teach!*

What a bunch of hooky the phycologist thought, she could tell just by looking at him that he was slower than molasses. "I said take it out," she repeated when Travis looked at her as though he didn't know what she was talking about.

"You can't leave that there," she frowned twisting her mouth in distaste as Travis removed the wad of gum from his mouth and placed it on the back of his hand. She pulled a tissue out of a box and used it to remove the wad of gum from the back of Travis' hand. She balled the whole mess up and threw it in the trash.

"That was mine," Travis looked at her with all the anger and hurt that had been building up in him for months.

The anger tore through his empty stomach like a bullet from an AK-47 rifle. Anger and hurt had been there jabbing at him since the second week that his Dad didn't come home, and it cut a little deeper each time his mother walked pass him and his brothers like they were less than nothing.

Travis had never directed his hurt and anger at any one person before because he blamed all of THEM. Except Miss Echols. Except Byron's Mom. Except Ma Turner. Except the people at the church that had given him the box of food and the coats.

Travis didn't exclude God. Byron's Mom told him about the just and merciful God that she served, but Travis never made a connection between that God and himself.

There was nothing just or merciful about having parents who weren't right. Parents who couldn't do the little things that most kids took for granted like coming home and making sure their sons had something to eat.

The woman throwing away his gum personified the general attitude of most of the adults around him. Nothing that belonged to him mattered. He and his brothers didn't matter. They were just another something to throw away.

He'd show her.

Another child who had lived a different life than the one Travis lived-one that respected and valued what adults thought of them- would have gone out of their way to impress the woman by showing her how smart they were. How free they were of intellectual disabilities. Not Travis.

He shut down.

He refused to answer any of her stupid questions. He was tired from keeping a nightly vigil to keep his brothers safe-never sleeping more than twenty minutes at a time. He was weak from months on limited rations.

It didn't matter to him which of the pictures matched or didn't match or which pieces completed a puzzle. What did it matter to him what an ink blob looked like?

The woman testing him, and first grade were a total waste of his time. If someone had told him that everything, he would ever need to know was taught in kindergarten, he would have quit school after kindergarten, stayed at home with Rodney and let Anthony come to school every day.

He knew his alphabet. He knew how to write his name. He knew colors, shapes, how to count and identify money. He knew what different animals looked like and what sounds they made, and how to cover his mouth when he coughed. He was trilingual speaking three languages- School English, Street English, and straight-up Hood English. He knew that it was polite to say please and thank you and he knew all about Helpers like farmers, nurses, doctors, and firemen.

What more could there possibly be to learn?

In fact, he decided to skip the rest of first grade, and he would have if not for the fact that school was now their major source of food.

He and Anthony took their bookbags to the cafeteria every day. It was amazing to them how much food other children wasted. Whole sandwiches, apples, bananas, tiny cartons of apple sauce and anything else that was headed for the trash was gladly collected and added to their small supply of food.

Travis and his brothers were getting by-making it until Christmas vacation. The whole concept of Christmas Vacation and another week off for the New Year didn't make a licking-bit-of-sense to Travis. Aside from the fact that they weren't learning anything new, Travis didn't see why they had to be out of school for nine whole days.

Anthony's class had a big Christmas party and all of the children in his class were given an 18inches long red Christmas stocking. The candy and fruit from the stocking and four bag lunches from the cafeteria supplied meals for the first five days. By the seventh day Travis was desperate.

Rodney cried all the time and Anthony complained every other minute about something. He wanted some real meat. He wanted some more food. The bread had mold on it. His head was hurting from all of Rodney's crying. He wanted his Dad to come back home. He wanted this. He wanted that. He wanted more than Travis could give him.

Chapter

6

Their mother came home on the fifth day of January. She was a hot mess. Her hair was matted with blood and sticking up all over her head. There was a knot on her forehead. Her right eye was swollen shut and her left eye had a black and purple ring around it. Her lower lip was so big that it looked like it was pregnant with twin lips.

She walked in, picked up Rodney and sat down with him on her lap.

"Well, aren't you going to tell me how much you missed me?" She looked at Travis, but she reached out to pull Anthony closer to her side. Her eyes seemed to dare either of them to comment on the way she looked.

"I missed you Mama. Especially your cooking," Anthony said.

Travis didn't say anything.

"Y'all know there's a notice on the door saying they're gonna put us out if the rent is not paid by the tenth. I'm gonna beat them to it though, I'm gonna…" She dozed off or passed-out. Travis never could tell the difference between the two.

Travis sat and watched his mother and little brothers sleep for a while then he must have dozed off too because the next thing, he heard was someone banging on the front door.

"Don't answer it," his mother said just as Travis reached the door.

"Lisa, it's me Maylene Trivett. Byron's Mom. I know you're in there. Open the door," She knocked even harder on the door,

Travis opened the door.

"Oh, Baby. I didn't know. I didn't know," Miss Maylene said as she pulled Travis into her arms hugging him tight. She knew he didn't like to be hugged, but she suspected that it was because he wasn't used to being hugged rather than not liking it.

She did it anyway and she was surprised that he not only let her hold on, but he also seemed to return the hug. His skinny little arms clung to her neck and she could feel moisture from his eyes soaking the shoulder of her dress.

"Lisa, what's going on over here. Someone called me and said they thought your pimp beat you up and you were bringing your mess back here. You know what happened to that Hasty girl and her family when she ran back home.

Mother, sisters, and three children got killed," Maylene finished with a look of disgust on her face. It was an unwritten, but well understood rule in the Hood- *Don't sell drugs from where you live and don't run home when you know someone is coming after you with a gun.*

"All y'all need to stop talking about what you don't know. It wasn't a pimp. It was Sam that did this to me. I went to that trailer park where he's staying. I begged him to come home and take care of us. Him and that white hussy he's staying with messed me up like this."

"You're saying Sam Burrell did this to you?" Byron's Mom asked. Her voice and the expression on her face made it clear that she didn't believe it any more than Travis did. They both could remember all the fights and every time the bruises and black eyes were on Sam Burrell.

"Didn't I just say it. Didn't I say Sam and that woman did it. I don't have any reason to lie," his mother came as close to pouting as she could with her bottom lip sticking out like it was part of a second face.

"Okay, the lady I used to work for has a friend who started a place for women who've been beaten up. I'll go over to Sara's house and call her," Maylene started for the door with Travis still in her arms.

"Put him down. You ain't taking my child anywhere. You get out of here with Travis and you'll forget about the rest of us," His mother got up. Put Rodney down and stood with her hands out.

It was a clear choice for Travis. Choosing family over anyone else was always easy. He left Byron's Mom's arms and walked pass his mother to sit next to Anthony. "I'll be right back," Maylene said as she rushed out. She came back twice to ask Travis' Mom questions. First, the people at the Genesis Shelter for Women asked whether or not she could make it safely to the Project's manager's office. Her answer was yes.

Then, they wanted to know if she would agree not to disclose the location of the shelter. She agreed that she would tell no one where the shelter was located. The final time Byron's Mom came back she wanted to know if there was anything that she could fix for them to eat before they walked over to the to the Project's Office Building.

Travis' Mom looked at him.

"Nothing. Not a damn thing," Travis said. He didn't apologize to Byron's Mom for cussing. In fact, he didn't realize that he'd cussed.

When Byron's Mom heard this, she didn't fuss. She didn't remind Travis about her no cussing rule. She left the house and went to several of their neighbors and came back with a quarter of a roll of unsliced baloney, a block of unsliced cheese, a loaf of bread, the end of a five-pound bag of sugar (about 2 cups) and two packs of Kool-Aid. She went into the kitchen and got busy making fried baloney and cheese sandwiches.

The smell of the baloney cooking reminded Travis of the country ham that one of his father's relatives from Virginia had brought for a family reunion when Travis was three. The meat was a little salty, but until today it had been the best smelling meal he'd ever eaten.

As soon as they finished eating, they walked over to the Turner Courts Management Office. While they were waiting, Byron's Mom explained, "Just go and get better. They have doctors and other people to help you get on your feet. We'll have a rent party and pay for a couple of month's rent, so you'll have a place to come back to."

She didn't say it, but the "other people" she mentioned were the ones that were supposed to help folks like their Mom get off drugs.

After about a thirty-minute wait, a plain white van pulled up. A heavy-set woman dressed like a man got out and opened the back of the van. Not only were the windows covered, but there was a divider between the front seats and the two backseats. With the other windows painted in, it was impossible to know where they were going.

Panic began to set in. Travis always noted landmarks. No matter where he went, he could find his way back home.

But he couldn't see anything. He wouldn't know how to get himself and his brothers back home.

The fact that their mother was with them wasn't comforting. Travis knew they couldn't count on her to keep them safe. It was only him to keep Rodney and Anthony safe and he couldn't see where he was being taken.

Travis jumped up and tried to open the back of the van, but there was no way to open it from the inside. He felt a scream coming up from deep in his chest and he thought he was holding it in until he heard his mother yell, "Shut-up that acting crazy Boy! Before I beat you like you belong to me."

He couldn't stop. He sat on the floor and banged on the door. It wasn't until the Woman Man driving the van pulled over to the curb, jumped out of the van, opened the back doors, and pulled Travis into the surprisingly comforting softness of her arms that he quieted down.

She frowned at Travis' Mom, "Lady, I don't care how you discipline your children back at your house, but we don't allow corporal punishment at Genesis. You hit him and he'll grow up just like his Daddy beating on women."

"Are you better now, Lil' Dude?" She asked Travis after staring his mother back into her seat. "I'll take him up front with me."

As she carried him to the front of the van and buckled him into the passenger seat, Travis looked around. He saw a Piggly Wiggly Grocery Store. He saw a Comerica Bank on one corner. He saw a school crossing sign.

His racing heartbeat slowed down even more as he took a deep breath.

He knew where he was. He could get himself and his brothers back home.

*   *   *

Travis would never forget that first night in the shelter. The room that the Woman Man took them to looked like a gymnasium and there were what looked like a thousand cots on every inch of the hard wood floor.

People were everywhere. Strange people were everywhere. Travis didn't know any of the people and the fact that the people were mostly women and children didn't make the fact that Travis didn't know any of them any easier on his nerves.

That first night went on forever. It seemed that every time he dozed off into one of his twenty-minute power naps; someone would wake up the whole place with nightmare screams.

"Stop, please stop."

"Help me. Somebody please. Please help me."

Besides the screaming and hollering, someone was up walking all night long. Travis was a light sleeper. The faintest sound woke him up on high alert. To Travis, faint sounds-tipping toes, whispering voices- meant someone was sneaking around. Faint sounds meant danger.

So, it wasn't that he was awake. He didn't need much sleep. He could stay awake all night if he had to. When he had to stay awake, he'd think and make plans for the next day. He'd practice counting money in large sums that he'd probably never get to hold. It was a restful kind of wakefulness.

Not that night. He couldn't rest. He had to stay wide awake just in case.

It was a long, long night.

As long as that first night had been, it wasn't a bad place. Travis and his brothers ate three meals a day. Three more than they'd had many days during the last six months. The Genesis Shelter for Women had some people who took care of the little children and tutored the school age children while their mothers went to something called counseling. Travis didn't know what counseling was, but he knew his mother didn't like it.

All evening after she came back from counseling she would grumble. Saying things like- "They act like they know me. They don't know anything about me. They're trying to get all up in my business."

They stayed in the shelter for eight days. The people begged their mother to stay longer, but she wouldn't stay, and she wouldn't allow the Shelter People to place the boys in Protective Custody.

The Genesis People took them back to Turner Courts and a couple of days later their mother left again.

Chapter

7

ravis was desperately hungry and bone and soul tired. He supposed that he was more tired and hungrier now than he'd ever been before because for a few shining moments yesterday he'd thought that the worst of their tribulation was over.

His mother came home again. This time she was all dolled up. Her reddish-brown hair the color of a pecan shell was long and shiny touching her shoulders with the ends curled under. Her make-up was on thick enough to hide the dark shadows that had been under her eyes for more years than Travis could remember. The red dress she wore had a smock turtleneck like a sweater and it fitted her close over her thin but still shapely body. Her five-inch black high heels were so thin that they looked lethal-to her if she tripped and to anyone she kicked.

The man she came in with had on one of the shiny suits that some pimps and street preachers wear. The pimps' suits were shiny because they wore suits made of what Ma Turner had called "shark-shin fabric and the street preacher's suits were shiny from being their only suit and being worn every day.

The man looked around. He frowned when his eyes settled on the coffee table where the small television that their father had gotten from a pawn shop used to be. It had been bare, since the third week after their Dad stopped coming home. What the man thought of what little furniture that was still there was clear from the prune like expression on his face.

There was a saying that- *Nothing put on the curb in Turner Courts was worth sh#@% cause when they threw something out it was 'Through'.*

The coffee-table was a testimony to that fact. One leg was taped together with electrical tape, there were scratches all over the table-top and both Travis and Anthony had practiced writing their names on it. The boys used the table as a catch-all for their candy wrappers, juice cartons, and empty lunch bags. The one lamp that remained had been glued and pieced back together every time it had been thrown at their Dad, but there was no hope for the lamp shade.

Travis and his brothers were huddled together on the only other piece of furniture in the room- a sofa that had been old when their Dad and one of his friends drug it in from the street.

The man looked at the boys and said, "Those two big ones are Sam Burrell's kids?"

"I told you that. Can't you see they look just like him, their Mom said.

"I ain't taking no kids of Sam Burrell nowhere. I ain't got no use for them. They ain't little enough to be cute. Get the one you came here for. I'll wait for you in the car," the man said as he walked out of the house.

Their Mom grabbed Rodney up. Ran to the bathroom and filled the tub with about three inches of water and washed him with the last of a bar of soap from her dresser. She dried him off with her bathrobe and dressed him in a new outfit from the bag she'd carried in with her.

"I'm taking Rodney with me. Y'all need to get Byron's Mom to take y'all over to your Daddy. He's living with a white woman on the other end of Spring Street."

Travis yelled at his mother's back as she left the house, "She can't take us nowhere. She isn't here anymore."

He thought his mother heard him because she slowed down a second, but she just shook her head a kept walking.

"Do you know where Spring Street is?" Anthony asked.

"It's one street up from where the Turner's Store used to be," Travis wasn't sure it was the right street, but he never admitted to being unsure about anything. Not to Anthony.

Anthony needed him to be sure about all the little things so that he would trust him on the big things when there wasn't time to explain.

"It's too deep into the night to go out there now. We'll go first thing in the morning," Travis didn't have to explain why going out too deep into the night wasn't safe. Anthony knew. A boy couldn't live too long in Turner Courts without figuring out when it was safe or at least close to safe to go out.

That night Travis slept almost all night. He only woke up when Anthony got up to go to the bathroom and he stayed awake until he laid back down.

The next morning, they didn't start out as early as Travis planned because Travis remembered something Miss Echols had said.

She said, "You can't control the condition or how many clothes you have but you can control how clean your clothes are."

Since then, Travis washed a few of their clothes with a couple of teaspoons of the soap-powder Byron's Mom had given him. There wasn't a full teaspoon left in the bottom of the box, but Travis ran some water in the tub and stirred the water around some. He twisted the clothes as hard as he could to get out most of the water. He used the community clotheslines to hang out the two shirts and two pairs of pants that he and Anthony wore interchangeably.

The coats that they had gotten from the church were the only items either of them claimed ownership of these days.

They had everything together.

They had nothing together.

The clothes were dry by mid-day. It was too warm to wear the coats because in was up into the mid-eighties by then. Winter days in Dallas were like that sometimes-like God forgot it was winter. The boys bundled their coats and their extra set of clothes into the wagon and started out to find their dad.

*   *   *

They were tired and they were the kind of hungry that introduces a boy's stomach to his backbone. The boys started taking turns riding in the wagon after the first mile or so, but they were about the same size. One of them pulling the other one along in the wagon slowed them down even more.

They stopped to discuss what to do. The way they saw it, they had two options. One, they could turn around and go back home- maybe their Mom would come back for them. Option two, they could leave the wagon and retrieve it on their way back.

Travis and Anthony were smart enough to know that neither option was feasible. They were too far away to get back home before dark and even their old rusted wagon would be gone within minutes if they left it on the side of the road.

The discussion did accomplish something. It gave them time to rest. They trudged on. By around four-o-clock that afternoon they were starting to see more and more white people.

They took turns asking the same question, "Do you know Sam Burrell? We're looking for our Dad.

Finally, when they came to a run-down house right outside a trailer park, a man said, "Could be. Why y'all out here looking for your Daddy?"

"Because we're hungry," Anthony said.

"Because our Mom told us to go find him," Travis said giving Anthony the mean eye for putting their business out there like that.

"Well, we've got plenty of food and I bet one of the guys will know which woman out here is living with a Nigga."

The boys stood there looking at each other trying to decide what to do. One of the first lessons they'd both learned was not to trust poor white people. The poorer they were the meaner they were. In the Hood there were no exceptions to the basic rules. Exceptions could get you hurt or killed.

In spite of the fact that the red truck in the front yard looked pretty good, from the looks of the house, Travis could tell that the man and anyone else living there had to be real poor. The porch was sagging and most of the top step was missing. The house looked like the Texas wind and rain had swept all traces of whatever color it used to be away and left it a tired grey that would drink up one hundred gallons of paint like molasses on a biscuit. They had to be poor to be living there.

Their Dad used to say, "The poorer white folks are madder with Colored folks, Mexicans and anyone else who's doing better than they are. They could have dropped out of school after failing eighth grade four times, but they'll still blame the fact that they can't get a good job on Colored Folks and Mexicans."

The man walked over and opened the front door. Travis and Anthony could smell the chili cooking and cornbread frying. That smell was like the Pied Piper of Hamelin to the boys. As they followed the smell and the man into the house, Travis remembered that he had not looked into the man's eyes to judge him as he usually did with adults, but as he grabbed Anthony's shoulder and turned to leave the man closed the door and stood in front of it.

This wasn't a house. Travis decided as he looked at the two desks on opposite sides of the front room. There was a grey metal filing cabinet next to one of the desks and the other desk held an old typewriter. One desk was as messy as the boy's coffee table back home and the other was as neat as Miss Echol's desk had always been.

Another man came from the back of the house. He was a big red bone man. In fact, everything about him seemed to be red. His nose was a red blob spread like a giant pus-filled pimple in the middle of his face. The shin of his face looked like red Play Dough˚ that had been left out of the container overnight.

"Well, well. Look what's Santa done sent us," the Red man's smile showed crooked and missing front teeth.

"I'm a gonna feed them first. You fix them something to drink. What flavor of Kool-Aid˚ do you boys like best? We've got all kinds," the man who'd brought them in asked.

"Red," Travis said.

"Purple." Anthony said.

The boys answered in unison. The Kool-Aide flavor of your choice was the only birthday tradition either boy could remember that made birthdays somewhat special in their family back in the days when their Dad came home. Travis' favorite was red-cherry and Anthony's was purple-grape.

While the Red man was fixing their Kool-Aide the other man gave each of the boys a bowl of chili and a hunk of corn bread. Travis watched the men while they ate. The man who brought them into the house didn't look anything like the Red man. The word that came to mind to describe him was long. His face was long with thin lips and squinty eyes that never opened enough for Travis to see what his eyes had to say about him.

"Here you go," the Red man said as he handed each of them a plastic container of Kool-Aide.

"I know. Tully always makes it too sweet," the Long man said when he noticed Travis frowning after taking a large gulp of the drink.

The drink wasn't too sweet to Travis. As far as he was concerned there was no such thing as too sweet when it came to candy or Kool-Aide. It was something else making it taste different, but he was too thirsty from their long walk to worry about it. He drank the whole thing.

He put the cup down. It felt heavy although it was empty. The piece of cornbread dropped to the floor.

Years later when he talked about, the time when he and Anthony were molested by those two white men; He could remember the pain. Not just his pain but Anthony's pain too because Anthony screamed and called for Travis to help him over and over again. And along with that pain there was a sense of shame and of failure as a big brother.

Chapter

8

"Inkie, did you see that? Those white men in that truck dumped something in that alley," Ham Bone said squinting his eyes to see better.

His eyes were as tired as the rest of his body. Over three hundred pounds of what once had been muscle was now mostly fat. Standing on his feet washing dishes all day at the restaurant where he and Inkie worked wore the big man out.

He'd played offensive lineman and defensive tackle all three years he'd been in tenth grade. It wasn't that he was too dumb to do the schoolwork. He just couldn't make it there enough days to equal the minimum attendance rule. "No, I didn't see nothing that looked like two naked boys and a wagon being dumped in that alley. And if you have a lickin' bit of sense you didn't see nothing either," Inkie was disgusted with the lack of feeling in his voice until he remembered why he didn't care anymore.

"I suppose they're dead but what if they ain't?"

"If they're dead and someone sees us coming out of that alley, you know who'll get blamed," Inkie knew about the eyes in the Hood.

He knew that even though he couldn't see them there were eyes peeping out from behind broken blinds and faded curtains. There were doors cracked open with only the chain of the lock protecting those inside. Someone always saw everything that went on. They might not say anything unless a big reward was posted for information or the crime hit too close to home, but NOTHING went unseen in the Hood.

Folks were always coming and going from somewhere. From their second or third job. From a booty call. To find their next fix. To sell someone their next fix. That end of the street looked deserted at 2:00 a.m. but Inkie knew better. Someone was watching.

Still Ham Bone hesitated.

"Man, you know Travis and Anthony are the only ones that be pulling an old wagon like that around. It's got to be them," Ham Bone made another appeal to his friend.

"You say all that to say what? If it's them and they're dead what good will it do them if we go to jail just cause you want to be noisy," Inkie said it like he didn't care whether they were dead or not, but Ham Bone knew him better than that.

Inkie's skin was inky purple black like Ivory Coast Blacks, thus the nickname that some guy had given him back in first grade. It was funny, but women saw him differently. To a discerning woman, the darkness of his skin emphasized the brightness of the teasing sparkle of his coal black eyes and the depth of the dimples in both cheeks. Dark as his skin was, there was nothing dark about his nature- at least it didn't use to be.

Inkie had always taken care of folks. He was forever going to the store for old folks and bringing them back all their change. He'd looked out for Ham Bone since they were about Travis and Anthony's ages. But all the caring changed when Inkie's younger brother was killed last year in a drive by shooting. Inkie had cried like a baby and it seemed to Ham Bone that every tear washed away a bit of the caring until it was all gone.

Inkie started walking down the street, "Man, you are coming?"

"I can't leave them like that," Ham Bone said as he headed toward the alley.

"Oh. Hell," Inkie turned around and followed him.

It's them, Ham Bone shouted although Inkie was less than a couple of feet away by then.

Inkie reached over and felt Travis' neck for a pulse.

"This one is still alive."

"This one is too," Ham Bone said as Anthony jerked away from his touch. His eyes never opened but his mouth opened as though he was preparing to scream.

"Don't do that.," Hambone covered his mouth. 'It's me Ham Bone. I ain't gonna let those men hurt you anymore," He held his hand over Anthony's mouth until Anthony quieted down as though he understood on some deep level that he was safe.

"What do we do with them now Mr. Hero Man?" Inkie wasn't ashamed to let his sarcasm show.

"We can't just take them home. I been hearing for a while that their Dad stopped coming home and their Mom leaves them alone for days. I guess we should take them to Miss Mae Ella."

"We can't go walking over there with them naked like this. Folks will think we're some kind of perverts or something."

"You reckon?" Inkie was disgusted that Ham Bone just figured that out. Both men removed their jackets and wrapped the boys in them.

"Look here. It's a grocery bag," Ham Bone said as he opened it. "Looks like a set of clothes."

"We ain't standing in this alley dressing them. It won't be long until the police get here. You know somebody called them when you shouted, IT'S THEM. Let's get out of here."

The men moved quickly to the path around the back of the building. They kept off the street using the backs of buildings as street markers.

*   *   *

"It's Ham Bone Miss Mae Ella." They'd gone around to her back door and Ham Bone knew how important it was to identify yourself when you went knocking at someone's door at two-o-clock at night.

"Ham Bone, Baby what you done got into now?" Miss Mae Ella called as they heard her shuffling to the door.

She knew all the people in the Hood. She'd been tending to them since before they were born. Giving their mothers some of her special teas to calm their stomachs or baths for sore swollen feet so they could keep working right up to the day their child was born.

"We got Travis and Anthony here. They've been hurt really bad. Where you want us to put them Ma'am? Inkie said.

"Lord. Lord. Put those Babies over here. They were all Babies to her. The men followed her into the front room of the little house and laid the boys on the cot that she used as an examination table.

"Who would do something like this to these children?" She exclaimed as she gently turned each of them over.

"All we know is that two white men in a red rusty truck drove up to the alley on Gee Street, jumped out of the truck, pulled them out naked from the back of the truck and threw them and the wagon in the alley. Then they took off."

"Why didn't y'all kill them?"

"They moved so fast that by the time we figured out what was going on they were gone," Ham Bone was quick to explain.

"More I think about it. They moved like they'd done this before kind of like when you practice a football play over and over," Inkie added. "Remember those run-away boys they found dead in an alley last year? They said they were naked too."

"Yeah but they were white boys and just because they found them near here it doesn't signify anything. That didn't have nothing to do with over here," Ham Bone didn't want to make a connection because if there was a connection maybe if they'd paid attention back then Travis and Anthony wouldn't have been hurt.

In spite of what happened back in 1954, Dallas was still pretty much segregated in 1986. Not as much by race but by economic circumstances. People of Color and white folks went to their own churches and lived mostly in their own neighborhoods. Black children and Mexican American Children went mostly to public schools and white children went mostly to private or Christian schools.

The story about those naked white boys being found just outside of Turner Courts was a big story until word got out that they were crackheads who'd come to the projects to buy drugs. Then, a tough looking white man with a red acne marked complexion and a nose that looked like it had been broken a couple of times told a reporter that he'd seen boys that looked like the ones that were found wearing dresses and make-up earlier that day.

That did it. The story, as far as the public was concerned, and the investigation died from lack of interest.

No one seemed to care about teenagers who were not only messed up with drugs but gay too. Folks said that no one would miss them except their mothers. Their mothers went on the news a couple of times declaring that people were lying.

*   *   *

The mother in a tank top that made her arms look like boiled ham hocks, said, "They were good boys. They'd just got work doing odd jobs at a Trailer Park. Two men in a red truck picked them up for work, day before yesterday. They wouldn't be caught dead over there on the Colored side of town. I couldn't see the men in the truck too good, but I could see that they weren't Colored."

A scrawny woman puffing on a cigarette said, "They weren't like what people are saying about them. They both have been playing football since they were five and both had girlfriends," the other teenager's mother said.

*   *   *

"Yeah, I remember what those mothers said. And I also remember that no one believed them when they couldn't name the trailer park or even tell where it was located. Anyway, mothers are always the first to know and the last to admit it when their sons are gay. I remember all that and just because it was a red truck that dumped Travis and Anthony it doesn't mean it was the same men." Inkie added all the facts up for Ham Bone and Miss Mae Ella.

"Man, I know there are about as many red trucks in Texas as there're horses, guns, and cattle. I'm just saying that it could mean something when we talk to the police."

"Ain't nobody talking to the police about nothing. We know that what happened to them didn't happen over here, but the Headlines would read,

BROTHERS 5 & 6 FOUND MOLESTED IN TURNER COURTS

We've got enough bad stuff being said about us right now. They're saying everybody over here are crackheads. They're saying all of us are on Welfare. They're saying we don't care about our children and they're saying that we're sitting around all day watching soap operas instead of cleaning our houses," it was easy to tell that, to Miss Mae Ella, the last insult was as low an insult as could be assigned to a Black woman.

She finished, "We don't need more of that and these boys don't need it either. They've been hurt enough. All of us are at fault too. We've been knowing for a long time that something needed to be done to help these boys. Y'all don't know nothing about this. Here's what you're gonna do…"

After that, she dressed the boys and patched them up as best she could. Then, she and Ham Bone waited with the boys until Inkie retrieved their wagon from the alley.

Miss Mae Ella instructed Inkie and Ham Bone,

"Y'all take the boys and their wagon back home. Leave the door unlocked. I'll take care of the rest," Miss Mae Ella didn't go into details.

Sometimes not knowing is better than knowing.

Chapter

9

Travis' eyes wouldn't open. He tried to open them earlier when he realized that the voices, he heard belonged to Inkie and Ham Bone. He knew he was safe with them, so he let the pain and the drug that the men had given him pull him back under.

"Travis! Don't be dead. Don't be dead," Travis woke with Anthony shouting in his ear.

He tried opening his eyes again. Although his eyelids felt like they weighed fifty pounds, he managed to get them opened enough to assure Anthony that he wasn't dead.

"We're at home Travis. Was it real? Was it a bad dream?" Anthony's eyes pleaded with Travis to confirm the lie.

"Yeah, that's exactly what it was. We must have slept the day away," Travis whispered his voice sounding low and hoarse.

Anthony nodded although both of them knew deep down that it was a lie. The bruises all over their bodies screamed liar, but both boys needed to believe the lie to survive.

Travis didn't know how long they sat on the couch leaning against one another for comfort. The blinds were always pulled down so no one could look in and the boys had no reason to look out.

They stopped looking out every time they heard someone outside after the second week that their father stopped coming home.

So, when Mr. Herman, Turner Courts Head Maintenance Man, and a strange lady walked in it was too late for them to run and hide. Not that they had the strength or the will to do any running or hiding.

"Where're your parents?" Mr. Herman didn't bother with amenities. He was a heavy-set man, but his thickness was solid. He bragged about serving under Frank E. Petersen the first African American Marine Corps aviator and the first African American Marine Corps general. Even though he had been a Marine, his job as the Complex's manager, required him to be harder on people than it was his nature to be, but he'd learned the first year on the job that his kindness was often taken for weakness.

From the boys, all he got as an answer to his question was a silent lifting of their shoulders.

"Well, if one of your parents isn't here, then there's nothing I can do to stop it. This lady is here to take y'all into protective custody. Do y'all know what that means?" He didn't wait for an answer. He picked both boys up by the scruff of their shirts.

"Don't handle them so roughly," the woman counseled.

"Roughly? From the looks of it they've been fighting each other and both of them lost." Mr. Herman laughed at his own pathetic joke.

Any other time, Travis and Anthony would have fought like a couple of pro-wrestlers anyone who handled them that way but that day-that day they just didn't care. As long as they were going together, they just didn't care.

As soon as Mr. Herman loaded both boys into the back of the woman's car, she knelt next to the open car door to put herself on eye level with the boys.

"I'm Miss Rivers you caseworker. Do you know what that means?" She paused waiting for a response. Neither boy said anything.

"It means that I'm going to take care of you. I'm going to make sure that you are in a safe and healthy place." Neither boy said anything.

"Well, you might not believe me but I'm going to prove you wrong," before getting into the car, she leaned over both boys checking their seatbelts.

Miss Rivers was tall for a woman, but more solid than thin. Although her skin was slightly sun-touched, and her hair was a thick, straight mixture of ten shades of brown it was impossible to determine whether she was black, Mexican, or white until she spoke. Her voice was the silky smooth, molasses sound of a Louisiana Creole.

Travis noticed that she smelled good. Not flowery- at least not like a rose which was the only flower that Travis could identify by sight. She smelled clean like Mrs. Echols used to smell. It was the fresh fragrance of Ivory Soap˚ and Mum˚ deodorant. Not so much any one smell. Just clean. For the rest of his life he would use that smell to label the women that he met.

*   *   *

The Buckner Baptist Children's Home was like another world to Travis. It had a lot of buildings, but those buildings weren't like the buildings in the projects that were identical in the simplicity of their design. Buckner Baptist Children's Home's buildings were as unique as the services that they provided. Miss Rivers talked to Travis and Anthony as she helped them from the car.

"First, we're going to clean you up and fit you with a weeks' worth of clothing-inside and out. You'll like that," she said. Then she answered herself, "I bet you will."

She'd stopped waiting for answers right after they got in her car, she observed them in the rear-view mirror, talking quietly to one another.

"If we're lucky we'll finish the intake process in time for you to get your lunch with the other children. They eat breakfast and dinner here, but every school day lunch is eaten at school."

She took them to a locker room with bathtubs and showers. The walls and floors were tiled in a gray and blue speckled tile. She tested the water after half filling the tub.

"I'm sure you boys can take it from here. I'll be back in twenty minutes with some clean clothes," she didn't try to help the boys undress because the woman who'd reported the abuse told them a little bit about the boys.

The woman had stressed the fact that the boys had been severely mistreated and as a result the older one was very protective of his younger brother. Frankly, she couldn't tell which one was younger, but she wanted to give them a chance to feel responsible for one another. The boys would need that closeness until they developed friendships with some of the other children. As a rule, the administration of the Home didn't encourage the children to become too attached to each other, but they did try to keep siblings together as much as possible.

She stood quietly on the other side of the room's partition listening to the boys.

"What's this place, Travis?" Anthony finally asked.

"One time, I heard Mama talking about that college that she went to. She said it had a lot of buildings. She called it a Campus. I think maybe that's what this is," Travis offered the best answer that he could come up with.

"A College Campus? Why they bring us to college when I ain't even finished kindergarten and you're still in first grade?" Anthony always had to keep digging for answers that Travis didn't have.

"Man, she always talked about that college when she talked about being a Gregory. Maybe, they brought us here because we're half Gregory. Forget about that. Let's just get in that tub before that lady comes back and tries to undress us and bathe us like we're babies," Travis put an end to the conversation.

The boys washed themselves like they always did.

More miss that hit. Then they washed each other's backs and stayed in the water waiting for the lady to come back.

"Here are a couple of towels. Dry yourselves off really good. We don't want you to catch colds," She turned her back while the boys dried off and got dressed. "You're going to have to talk to me and I know you both can talk. I heard you talking to each other a while ago," she stood there patiently staring them down.

After about five minutes, she added, "I've got all day, but those kids have been playing and working pretty hard since breakfast. So, I can't promise that there will be enough left over for you to get lunch if you take too much longer to start talking." She only had to wait five seconds for Anthony to break the silence.

"What you want to know?" Anthony wasn't about to miss out on a real meal.

"Just some basic stuff like your full names, ages, birthdays, mother's name, father's name, where you attended school, what grade you are in-stuff like that."

She ran down the list slower this time and the boys took turns answering as she made notes in a tablet. She walked with them over to the Clinic where they were weighed and checked out by the nurse.

"Now, to get something to eat," she said as she led them to the Cafeteria, "I was kidding when I said there might not be enough left for you to eat. There is always plenty of food."

Although she smiled when she said this, it was a strategic error for someone with her experience to make when dealing with boys like Travis and Anthony. They didn't see any difference between teasing and lying. Not when adults did it. They'd been easing to the point of letting their guard down with her, but as soon as she admitted to lying to them about the food, they mentally placed her back into the column of adults who couldn't be trusted.

It took her nearly all of the six months that they lived in the Buckner Home for Children to win back their trust. She promised to make time to spend with them every day. And she did. Sometimes on the weekdays it was just long enough to play a couple of games of checkers with them. Other times like on the weekends, she spent a couple of hours with them-eating lunch with them in the cafeteria and taking them to the playground. It didn't matter where they went or what they did. What mattered was that she kept her word.

Chapter

10

The first foster home was not a good fit for Travis and Anthony. In the first foster home, the family's name was Wadley, or something like that. It wasn't that big a house, but every room was stuffed with a hodgepodge of mix-matched furniture. That first foster home didn't work out because the couple's teenage son looked just like one of the men who'd messed with them.

He had pimples on his face that looked like Red Hots˚ that had been stepped on and he was forever picking at the pimples and making them bleed. After the first couple of days, the Wadley's son and his parents decided that the boys were funny or something because they kept holding on to one another and finding places to hide whenever the son was around. No amount of coaxing would entice them to come out of hiding until the son drove away in his truck.

Another problem, with the Wadley's house was that the room where they slept had three bunk beds and all the top bunks were taken. Any boy or man who's had to share a room with other boys or men knows how important it is to have a top bunk.

Enough said.

Since the Wadley's really needed the extra income from keeping foster children, they put up with the boys for two months.

The next foster home didn't work out either because Mrs. Keel, their second foster parent, felt that given their background, the boys needed to be watched all the time very carefully. According to her, the other three foster kids in her home came from a good Christian home. Their parents who'd been killed in an automobile accident on their way to church were surely in heaven watching over their children. But she was sure that the opposite was true of Travis and Anthony because of their response to her question, "What did Jesus die for?"

To which Travis said, "It was probably a bad drug deal."

Then Anthony put in his two cents worth, "Nah, it was probably a drive by shooting." Inkie's brother had been one of his best friends. So, naturally even two years later his death was fresh in Anthony's mind.

All the children at the Buckner Baptist Home went to church, but Travis and Anthony used the time in church for nap time. Their day to day lives had been so hard, that the entire concept of a loving God seemed as abstract to them as quantum physics. To boys who had spent most of their childhood sleeping on cold hard floors, burning in hell didn't seem so bad.

Both boys had perfected the fine art of appearing to be awake while sleeping rather soundly. They'd sit next to one another each one propping the other one up. To hide the fact that they were sleeping, both of them would use their outside hand to place a thumb under their chin and the other fingers over their eyes.

Mrs. Keel was shocked at the boy's responses. She decided right then and there that they were heathens with no hope of redemption. She was going to watch them every minute of every hour. To her mind, it was her God given duty to prevent the boys from turning out to be serpents encouraging the other children to do sinful deeds.

Lord knows she tried to do precisely that-to watch them every minute of every hour. She failed because she couldn't get enough sleep to watch them past eight o'clock at night. Every time she checked on Travis during the first three nights, Travis and Anthony were with her; Travis' big light brown eyes were wide open, looking right back at her. She gave up on them after three weeks.

The third time they were placed in foster care was the charm. They were finally placed in the right foster home with the right foster parent about six months after they were taken from their parents. Travis decided the first time he saw their new foster parent that she was a cross between Ma Turner and Miss Echols with a trace of Byron's Mom.

Miss Woodlock. That was her name. She was a Special Education teacher at the boys new school. In looks, she didn't remind Travis of anyone he'd ever known. She was tall for a woman-around 5'9in. but she wasn't skinny like Mrs. Keel had been. She had what the older guys back in his neighborhood would have called a rockin' shape with curves in all the right places. Her hair was the deep reddish brown of very fair skinned Black women.

Miss Woodlock's house was in a section of Dallas called Bonton. This was where a lot of wealthier or upper middle-class African Americans lived in South Dallas, Texas. It is bounded by Hatcher St. and Southcentral Expressway to the North and

West, respectively, and goes as far as Municipal St. and Donald St. to its East and South. Lauren Woods and Cynthia Mulcahy, artists/researchers, determined in their Dallas Historical Parks Project, that the name "Bon Ton" is possibly derived from the French expression "bon ton," which means high class in French. Miss Woodlock later told the boys that the house was the first and only house her parents owned. It was a totally new way of life for Travis and Anthony.

*   *   *

Because of the report that the school's psychologist put in his cumulative folder, Travis was labeled with a Learning Disability and put in Miss Woodlock's class when they started school while at Buckner Baptist Home for Children. For years, the Home had their own private schools on campus, because they were run by the Baptist and they had children from different races at the school. Schools in Texas were segregated until 1968. By the time Travis and Anthony got there in 1986, all the Buckner Baptist Home's children went to public schools.

Travis was never sure why Anthony was placed in Special Education. He guessed it was either because they had the same parents or maybe it was because having something wrong with your brain was catching like a cold or measles. That made more sense to Travis because he and Anthony had been sharing beds and diseases since they were babies.

At first, Travis didn't mind being placed in special education because the work was so easy that he could finish a day's work in ten minutes and spend the rest of the day building with the Legos or looking through the Jet magazines that Miss Woodlock kept in the Reading Center for the fifth grade boys or helping Anthony with his work.

After a while though, he was bored. Miss Woodlock started sending him to one of the regular second grade classes for math. By the Holiday Break, Travis was spending most of the day in a regular class.

Miss Woodlock didn't know it, but she started out on Travis' A-List and kept moving up. Her first 100 came when she showed the boys to their room. Instead of the cowboy and Indian theme that Byron's Mom had on his bedspread and curtains, Miss Woodlock had dark blue twill bedspreads and curtains. The walls were covered with posters of Michael Jordan, Darryl Strawberry, and Jerry Rice.

"This used to be my brother's room when he was growing up, but Mama and I took all his stuff out and fixed it up for you two. The whole family came over last weekend and helped paint and get the room ready. I hope you like it?" She ended with what sounded like a question.

"We'll take the bed near the wall," Travis didn't know what else to say. He liked the posters, but the room looked almost too nice to sleep in and the door didn't have a lock. Would she get upset if they messed up the beds or left their clothes on the floor?

"No. You don't understand. One bed is for you and the other is for Anthony. I guess he won't mind if you take the one next to the wall. Do you mind if Travis takes the bed near the wall?"

Anthony didn't say a word.

"All right then," she continued as she walked over and placed the bundle of belongs that were labeled as belonging to Travis on the bed next to the wall. "It's about time for dinner. We'll go wash up and you can help me set the table."

*   *   *

If this was what doing things "right" meant, Travis didn't ever want to be wrong again.

After they'd washed their hands, she showed them how to do something called setting the table. Everyone got a plate, a fork, a knife, a spoon, and a cloth napkin. There was a separate drawer for everything that went on the table in something she called a sideboard. She showed them where to put each item. Then she explained that this setting the table had been a chore that she and her sister shared, but now Rodney and Travis would do it.

A lady who she introduced to Travis and Anthony as her Mother set at the head of the table and placed the rice, string beans, and meatloaf on their plates when Miss Woodlock passed the plates to her. Then, she passed around the biscuits and told the boys to take one, but if they wanted another one after they finished that, they could get another one. After that night, they sat down together for dinner every weeknight and Saturday.

Travis thought that Miss Woodlock looked pretty good for an older woman. He figured she was about Bryon's Mom's age. He wondered why she didn't have a husband until he walked in on her one evening after he and Anthony were supposed to be in bed. It was Valentine's Day and she was sitting on the sofa with a photo album on her lap with tears rolling down her cheeks. Travis decided that he wasn't really thirsty after all and almost went back to bed. She wasn't a huggee-kissy person like Byron's Mom. Travis wasn't either. So, Travis didn't know what to do or say.

Finally, he sat down next to her and asked, "Who's that?" as he pointed to a picture of a man in an Army uniform.

"He was my fiancée. He asked me to marry him on Valentine's Day but while I was busy looking for the prettiest wedding gown and planning the biggest wedding ever held in this town, he was drafted and sent to Vietnam. He died over there."

"Why didn't you marry someone else since you already had the dress?" In Travis' experience boyfriends and girlfriends were interchangeable. Hadn't his Mom replaced his Dad with one man after another.

"I never found another Jonathan. I can't honestly say that I ever went looking. You'll understand what I mean one day. Let's go to bed. Tomorrow is a school day."

She walked with him down the hall. When they reached the boys' room, she turned to leave then turned back around and hugged Travis saying, "Thanks for caring." She was surprised when he hugged her back.

*　　*　　*

On some Saturday's they went out to dinner. Not to places like Sadie's Chicken Shack in their old neighborhood where people stood in line to get their food then took it home to eat, but in actual restaurants where they could sit down and eat. They ate at places like Smokey John's, located on the corner of Lemmon Street and Mockingbird Street. The menus said, BEST HOME COOKING ANYWHERE.

The food was Sho'nuff good, especially the barbecue, but Travis didn't see how that claim could be true since none of the people he saw there had ever eaten any of Byron's Mom's food. For sentimental reasons, he would always declare that her food was the best he'd ever eaten.

All the waitresses at Smokey John's and the other restaurants they went to seemed to know Miss Woodlock and her mother.

The waitresses would make over Travis and Anthony calling them the cutest little things. The boys would both roll their eyes like they didn't like it, but deep down they both loved getting all that attention.

Sunday's were the most special days of all. They went to church every Sunday. Not just to the regular service, but to Sunday school and Bible Band too. It was the Sunday School and Bible Band that finally made Church make sense to Travis. In the children's Sunday School classes, they talked more about the goodness of Jesus and made heaven sound like a place he might want to go to one day.

When they got back from church, Grandma Woodlock, that's what she told the boys to call her, would cook the main meat and dessert and Miss Woodlock, her sister, and her brother's wife would cook the side dishes and bread.

The whole family would sit down for Sunday dinner. Although the children ate at a small table over to the side, they still felt included because when one of the adults asked about their week, all the talking would stop at the big table. The adults actually listened to what the children had to say.

To Travis, this was one of the best things about Miss Woodlock. She talked to them and listened to them. She encouraged the boys to ask questions.

When she didn't know an answer, she'd say, "We'll find the answer together. It will be a learning experience for all of us."

Although the boys made up their mind not to mess up the good thing they had there. Since they were still technically children, they messed up a few times.

One time, Anthony got in trouble for taking a kid's lunch. He swore out that he'd asked the boy very nicely if he was going to finish his sandwich and when the boy said, "I don't want it." Anthony ate it. Since it was Anthony's word against the other boy's Travis and Anthony were sure that he wouldn't be believed.

Miss Woodlock surprised them. She told the teacher,

"I believe Anthony. You believe Tim. If Tim is still hungry. I'll pay for another sandwich. What we're not going to do is punish Anthony based on one student's word," then she took Anthony by the hand and led him back to class.

"Are you still hungry," she asked Anthony after they entered her class.

'No Ma'am. I'm full," Anthony said in his usual polite way.

"Did your parents teach you to say Yes Ma'am and No, Ma'am like that?" As often as she could, she tried to find something positive about their parents to help them remember the good over the bad.

"No, Ma'am Travis said to say it to grownups who don't get high or use drugs. We figured you didn't when you dressed up to go to that party and didn't come back drunk."

"How did you know I wasn't drunk? It was well after midnight when I got in."

"Oh, Travis was awake. He always is. He said that the man you went out with didn't have to carry you down the hall to your room and he heard you stop by your mother's room to tell her that you were back and that you talked to her awhile. He said you didn't sound drunk or high." Anthony finished his narrative as though he and Travis had drawn their conclusion about her sobriety in the most scientific manner.

"I suppose Travis is an expert on whether or not grownups are sober or drunk," she said it jokingly.

"Had to be," Anthony was dead serious. He didn't go on to explain about the necessity of knowing the condition of the adults around you when you're growing up in Turner Courts Projects.

Miss Woodlock smiled, but she didn't laugh.

* * *

After that, Travis and Anthony thought they would make it to the end of the year without any more mess-ups.

They doubled up on their Yes, Ma'ams and No, Ma'ams and Please and Thank-u's. Things were going well. Then Travis got in trouble and it was far more serious than the offense of which Anthony had been accursed.

The Teacher's discipline referral said:

Name: *Travis C. Burrell*
Date: *January 14, 1988*
Offense: *Travis was highly disrespectful to the teacher. He called me a liar. Talking back and refusing to apologize to the class*
Teacher: *Mrs. Horner*
Grade: *2*

"How could you?" Miss Woodlock didn't wait for an answer. "How could you say that to a teacher?" She didn't yell, but she put balled-up fists on her hips and stared him down.

"Because she was lying," Travis said.

"What do you mean by that?" Miss Woodlock looked puzzled like she'd never called anyone out for lying.

"She was lying," Travis repeated as though that statement explained everything. He refused to say anything else.

His refusal to talk about the details of the incident, left Miss Woodlock with no alternative but to go along with the punishment; five days out of school suspension and canceling his birthday party that was planned for January 17th.

A few days after Travis' birthday, Miss Woodlock overheard Mrs. Horner talking about the incident in the Teacher's Lounge. If Miss Woodlock hadn't been saved sanctified and filled with the precious Holy Ghost, she would have slapped Mrs. Horner from one end of Texas to the other end.

Mrs. Horner confided in her friend that she had welcomed her students back from their Holiday Break by saying, "I know that Santa Claus was really good to all of you because Santa makes sure good little boys and girls have a wonderful Christmas."

Travis said, "That's a lie. If your Dad didn't bring some money home no matter how good you'd been you wouldn't get anything."

Travis and his brothers had learned the truth about Santa Claus the hard way. Although there were charity organizations that tried to ensure that even the poorest of children got at least one gift for Christmas, their Mother stood fast on the fact that Gregory's didn't take charity from anyone.

Then, Mrs. Horner told her friend, "And when I insisted that Travis apologize to the class he flat out refused saying, "I ain't lying to these children. Can you believe that?"

"Oh, I can believe it. Those children from that home shouldn't be allowed to be around innocent little children," her friend, Miss Johns said.

At this point, Miss Woodlock had to put in her two cents worth, "I honestly can't believe that you wrote a discipline referral on that child for telling the truth. Maybe he could have put it another way, but he is just a child. When they asked me about Santa Claus, I told him and Anthony that it was something small children enjoyed at Christmas time. They've seen too much of "real life" to believe in fairytales. Any adult with an ounce of compassion," she paused to stare at both of them contemptuously, "Any Christian would not blame children for their parents faults," she didn't wait to hear what they had to say. She turned and left them with their mouths open.

Miss Woodlock stopped at the bakery and got Travis a belated birthday cake. He smiled when he blew out the candles, but it wasn't the same.

Chapter

11

She thought they were cute. No one had ever said that about Travis or Anthony. Rodney was the cute one. Their father was the handsome one. Never Travis or Anthony. But Miss Woodlock thought they were cute.

Miss Woodlock liked what she called their caramel colored eyes. Their mother had cursed their eyes especially those last few months before they were taken away from her, because she said they were their Dad's eyes. She said their eyes were lying cheating eyes. It seemed to Travis and Anthony that all the love she'd felt for their Dad had festered into a canker sore where her heart used to be.

Miss Woodlock said she loved it when they laughed because the first few months that they were with her they never smiled or laughed. She even discovered that they both had a dimple in their right cheek. She dressed them as though they were twins and she enrolled them in a modeling class. Although they would have rather been playing Pee Wee Football or basketball like some of their classmates, they didn't complain because modeling meant getting new outfits every month.

In one modeling show, they wore jackets like the one Michael Jackson wore in the Thriller video. The jackets weren't pleather, plastic that looks like leather, like most of the guys that wore Thriller jackets had but real soft as butter leather and their matching pants were real leather too. When they modeled the outfits in a show, they came out doing the final dance from the Thriller video. Every time they performed that dance the whole crowd stood up and gave them what Miss Woodlock called a *standing ovation.* Travis and Anthony were the undisputed stars of every fashion show. The standing ovation meant that the crowd really, really liked them.

Travis would watch the people slapping each other on the back and giving each other high-fives like they had something to do with the boy's performance. Maybe they did. Hearing those people applaud made them feel something that they had never felt before. Accepted. Accepted for who they were no matter where they'd come from.

Travis didn't think that those people understood how much that form of tacit approval meant to him and to his brother. People who had never been looked down on just couldn't understand. The uproarious applause meant acceptance of them as people of worth. They knew that they had that from Miss Woodlock and Grandma Woodlock, but acceptance from those two was kind of a given. They were nice ladies who had brought the boys into their home and kept them there for almost a whole year.

It was that kind of acceptance that they had expected but never received from Mrs. Keel or from the Wadley's. The boys had good reason to expect acceptance from their foster parents because everyone knew that children who had been removed from their parent's home had been through some bad stuff. Bad stuff that wasn't their fault-that they didn't have any control over. Miss Lewis had shared with the boys a pledge that all foster parents had to learn and told them that their foster parents would do exactly what they had pledged to do before God and their Foster Parent's Training Instructor. The pledge went like this:

In our home and foster family, I/we believe all members-regardless of age, gender or ancestry-always have equal rights to:

1. Have their ideas, feelings and dreams heard and respected.
2. Have their needs considered seriously and fairly.
3. Know clearly who' s responsible for what, and what our rules and consequences are.
4. Make and learn from their own mistakes without shame or excessive guilt.
5. Be seen as a unique, special, and worth-while person .
6. Learn and grow at their own pace and in their own direction.
7. Enough privacy, space, and freedom of choice.
8. Protection from family members who abuse, neglect, share, or violate personal boundaries.
9. Unconditional love, respect, and physical, emotional, and spiritual safety.
10. Their own friends, values, and activities, as long as they are not harmful, in the judgment of the foster parents.

Travis and Anthony decided that the Wadley's and Mrs. Keel crossed their fingers behind their backs when they took the pledge.

Miss Woodlock couldn't make all the bad stuff go away, but she did push it out of the boy's everyday lives. They weren't hungry every day. They weren't afraid every day. They didn't have to take care of themselves or worry about being left to fend for themselves. And most of all they had an adult who was on their side.

Not only was Miss Woodlock on their side. She kept them by her side when she left home.

She called it a vacation. This was an entirely new concept to Travis. In Turner Courts, the people who worked, worked all the time. Because Miss Woodlock refused to fly, she took them from Dallas to Los Angeles by train. Although it was a more than 12-hour trip they were never bored. There was too much to see.

She only got upset with Travis one time when she woke up and couldn't find him. It took her ten frantic minutes to locate him in the Dining Car. Even though she didn't yell, she gave him the mean look that she only used at school with her worst discipline problems.

Travis heard her calling his name and when he looked away from the window all he saw was the mean face with her eyes half closed and her face all crunched-up.

She said, "Boy, I can't sleep when you won't. It's not as bad as it used to be, but this train is different. If you left the house during the night on our street, my phone would be ringing off the hook before you got to the corner. Didn't I ask you to stay close to me at all times?"

If it had been any other adult, Travis would have played it off pretending that he asked her, and she'd grunted something that he mistook as "yes."

But this was Miss Woodlock.

So, he told her the truth, "I waited until I knew you were asleep. I wanted to see out from the Dining Car. When we were in here for dinner, the waiter said that it has the best view on the train at night. I thought I'd be back before you woke-up."

She started crying and pulled him into her arms, "My God Travis, I thought I'd lost you. I thought that maybe you'd fallen off the train. I thought that someone had grabbed you and taken you off the train."

He knew her tears weren't fake ones like his mother used to get what she wanted. He could feel the wet from her eyes against his cheek. "I'm sorry Ma'am. I didn't mean to scare you."

"It's all right. If you'd been kidnapped Anthony and I would have chipped in together to get you back." Trying to laugh at this inside joke, she used a napkin to dab at her eyes. Both of them knew that Anthony took being stingy to a new level. Miss Woodlock had started giving them something called an allowance. At first, they thought it was payment for doing their chores, but she set them straight.

She said, "Doing your chores is your contribution to the family. Your allowance is to help you learn how to manage and save your money."

Anthony got the saving part really good. Grandma Woodlock, always said, "That boy squeezes a dime so tight that it has blisters on it."

So, Miss Woodlock and Travis knew that if getting Travis back from kidnappers required money from Anthony the kidnappers would have had to keep him.

"Travis, I'm tired. Will you do me a favor and go to sleep?" She smiled when she said this.

"Yes, Ma'am. Travis smiled back and he did finally go to sleep.

Everything else about their vacation was perfect. They went to Disneyland and all the other tourist sights, but Travis' favorite place was New Ladera Heights where there were amazing custom homes owned by rich and famous Black people like baseball player Frank Robinson. One of Miss Woodlock's cousins lived in one of the largest houses. Miss Woodlock told them as they toured her cousin's house, "I wanted you to see how far you can go if you're willing to work hard and stay out of trouble. My cousin came here from Mississippi with his parents. They were dirt poor.

He watched his father working taking care of rich folks' gardens. He watched and worked hard and learned everything there was to learn about gardening. Now his business makes millions of dollars every year."

"Work hard, watch and learn, and stay out of trouble," Travis thought to himself. "I can do that."

*   *   *

Travis would never forget the night that Miss Woodlock told them that she wanted to adopt them. After they got in from school, she told them to put on one of their Sunday suits because they were going out for a special dinner celebration.

Travis and Anthony were puzzled. As long as they'd been with her, she'd stressed the fact that school clothes were for school, and church clothes were for church. By default, the clothes that had been given to them at the Buckner Baptist Home for Children became their play clothes.

What could be so special that Miss Woodlock would allow them to wear their Church clothes out to eat? Even when they had Sunday dinner with the family, they changed out of their Church Clothes.

As they changed out of their school clothes into their Church Clothes, the boys tried to puzzle through the problem together.

"What do you think this is about Travis?"

"It can't be anything good, because Grandma Woodlock isn't coming with us," Travis was just as puzzled as Anthony. He'd almost stopped expecting something bad to happen. Once in a while, he'd wake up in the morning and realize that he'd slept the whole night through.

When they got to the restaurant instead of the waitress taking them to a table or booth, she led them to a large dining area on one side of the restaurant.

Everyone was there. Grandma Woodlock, Miss Woodlock's sister and her husband and their two children and her brother and his wife and their three boys and all the rest of their extended family was there. Miss Rivers was there, and Byron and his mother were there.

Everyone stood up and shouted, "Surprise!"

The brothers were more than surprised. They were shocked. It wasn't either of their birthdays. It wasn't what happened when they were being sent back to Buckner's. They knew that routine. During the school day, both times that they'd been sent back, right after lunch, they would both be called up to the office and Miss Rivers would be there waiting to take them back to Buckner's she would have collected their things from their foster parent's house. Miss Rivers always made it clear that it wasn't their fault that they were being sent back to Buckner's Baptist Home for Children.

No, there were no surprises there.

"What are we supposed to be surprised about?" Travis got up enough nerve to ask.

"It's one of the most special and exciting things that's ever happened to me." Miss Woodlock beamed. "I hope you'll feel the same way." She turned to speak to the waitress. "We have a reservation for the banquet hall."

Travis and Anthony looked at Miss Woodlock as if to say, "We still don't get it."

"Travis and Anthony, I didn't want to say anything until the year was up. In the state of Texas, natural parents have a full year to file petitions to have their children returned to their care. If they don't. A foster parent can petition the court to adopt the children. It's been one year and 10 days. I filed the papers to adopt both of you. I want you to be my sons. I want to be your Mama," She paused and looked at them as though she was waiting for an answer.

When neither boy said anything, she prompted, "Well, do you want me to be your Mama?"

Travis looked at Anthony and Anthony looked at him. Travis could tell that they were thinking the same thing. They'd had a Mama and that didn't work out very well. Their Mama didn't like the way they looked, especially their eyes. Miss Woodlock did. Their Mama didn't spend any time playing with them or talking to them. Miss Woodlock did. Their Mama didn't seem to like them very much. Miss Woodlock made them feel loved. Nope, they didn't want or need another Mama. They wanted Miss Woodlock.

"Will you still be Miss Woodlock?" Anthony put their feelings into words.

"Oh, I see. Yes, I will still be Miss Woodlock. That will never change, but I'll be more. You will be my sons and you will live with me permanently."

"That's all right then," Travis said. After a brief conference with Anthony, he announced, "After you adopt us, we'll call you Mama Woodlock.

Anthony started calling her Mama Woodlock the next day.

She smiled when he called her Mama Woodlock, but deep down she prayed that one day both boys would just call her Mama and that they would love her as much as she loved them.

*   *   *

They had to wait six more months for the adoption to be final. It was 5:30p.m. of the day after the last day of the sixth month. No one had come forward to stop the adoption.

This was the big day.

After an early dinner, they were going to the attorney's office to sign some papers. Both boys had been practicing signing their names. It was Anthony's turn to pick the place where they would eat out. He picked Chuck E. Cheese.

"Really, Anthony? You can be such a baby sometimes." Travis was thoroughly disgusted with this choice. He was nine and didn't feel like spending an evening with mostly three and four-year-olds and hearing "Happy birthday to You" sung a thousand and one times.

"It's his turn Travis. Anthony and I weren't too thrilled with your choice of that pizza place last time, but we went along peacefully."

She gently squeezed Travis' shoulder. It was her way of reminding him of his responsibility as a big brother. As she always said, "Big brothers helped younger brothers feel good about themselves."

"Okay, I guess it's all right. Good job Anthony," Travis looked up at Miss Woodlock for approval.

She smiled. That smile had come to mean so much to Travis during the last year and a half. She wasn't stingy with her smiles, but it was the way her eyes lit up that made the person on the receiving end of a great big Miss Woodlock smile feel as though he meant something to her. That he was special.

Chapter
12

They went to a table and after ordering their food. Miss Woodlock gave each of them a handful of tokens and the boys went to play arcade games.

Travis liked most of the things about Miss Woodlock's theory of what a big brother should do for his younger brother. He liked that though he was expected to look out for Anthony, he wasn't held responsible for every aspect of his care.

For the first time in his life he was beginning to feel like a kid. Yes, he liked everything about her theory of big brotherhood except one thing: Letting Anthony win sometimes to help build his confidence. To Travis, there was never a good reason to lose. A person, even a younger brother, should only win if he worked hard enough to be the best.

He'd beaten Anthony at two games when Anthony shouted, "Travis there's a police officer over there messing with Mama Woodlock."

"Man, you are not about to get me to look away from this game with that mess," Travis didn't bother to look up. Anthony would try any trick to win.

"I'm not lying. It looks like she's crying." His voice broke on a sob as he ran to help her. Travis passed him before he'd made three steps. When they got to her Travis took a protective stance next to her looking at the policeman. But Anthony threw himself into her arms.

For Anthony's sake, Miss Woodlock tried to pull herself together. "It's going to be all right. We'll call Miss Rivers and get this straightened out."

The policeman said, "It's straightened out. The boys, my sister's sons, are going to North Carolina with me to be reunited with their mother. I have the papers releasing them into my custody."

Miss Woodlock took the papers and tried to make sense of what she was reading. The papers said that the man was John Gregory and that their mother had been to a drug rehab center and moved back to High Point, North Carolina. The Guilford County Department of Social Services had presented her petition to regain custody of Travis C. Burrell and Anthony B. Burrell to the Child Protection Court of the Dallas County Department of Social Services over six months ago. Her petition had been granted two days ago.

"I don't understand how this could happen. I've checked with their social worker, Miss Rivers every day for the last three months because I didn't want to get our hopes up if there was any chance of the adoption not going through. Why didn't someone let me know. Let them know?"

"Ma'am, I can't answer that. Somebody here must have dropped the ball, but we'll have to leave now if we're going to board the plane in time."

"Now? You're taking them now?"

"Yes, Ma'am. Right now. I lost a couple of hours driving over here from your house in five-o-clock traffic."

"I need to pack their things. I need to let the lawyer know that we won't be there to sign the adoption papers. I need to let Mama know what's happened. I need…'

"I don't have time for that Ma'am," he cut her off. "We have plenty of clothes at home that my boy has outgrown. Come on boys. Anthony stop acting like a big old baby."

He pulled Anthony off Miss Woodlock's lap and signaled for Travis to follow him.

Travis didn't say anything.

He remembered the man from a scrapbook that used to be on the coffee table in their living room. Every once in a while, his mother would pick it up and show them pictures of her big brother, their uncle John Gregory. A couple of pictures were newspaper clippings from when he was a star player on a high school football team. There were also pictures of him as a police cadet, but her favorite one was the picture of him taken in 1983 with him in uniform standing next to his police car.

The summer before his Dad had stopped coming home there was a big uproar over the possibility that someone in their Hood was working undercover with the cops. Some brothers who'd run a legitimate looking automobile repair shop as a cover for their chop-shop for stolen cars were suddenly arrested and the ice cream truck that had supplied pot exclusively to South Dallas for years got raided.

There was a narc on the inside. There had to be. When a large reward was offered. Everyone and their Mama was suspect.

Travis' Dad had convinced his mother that having connections to a police officer, even one in another state was nothing to brag about. The scrapbook disappeared from the coffee table and their mother never again mentioned her oldest brother the big-time cop in High Point, North Carolina.

Travis started to follow his uncle, but when he looked back and saw that Miss Woodlock was sobbing so hard that her shoulders were shaking, he rushed back to her and wrapped his arms around her neck.

He whispered, "Don't cry. You can adopt some other boys. I know there're some other boys out there who would be proud to call you Mama,"

He tried to sound strong, but his heart was breaking because any boys she adopted wouldn't be him and Anthony.

"Go on son. You and Anthony will always be the only sons I ever had. Go on. I'll call my brother to come drive me home. Go on. You don't want him to take Anthony and leave without you?" She straightened her shoulders and wiped her eyes. She knew Travis well enough to know that he wouldn't leave her until he was sure she was going to be all right.

He stepped back and looked at her for a moment. He wasn't fully convinced, but he was afraid that his uncle would leave with Anthony.

She nodded once more and whispered, "Go."

Travis turned again to leave as she waved him away. He didn't look back.

His Uncle John was standing next to a rental car. He put Travis and Anthony on the back seat as though they were under arrest.

That's exactly how Travis felt. As though they were under arrest. As though he and Anthony had done something really bad. Try as hard as he could, Travis couldn't think of anything either of them had done that deserved to have something this bad happen to them. He could sympathize with the way

Adam must have felt when he got put out of Eden. The only difference was that Adam knew what he had done to mess up his good thing.

As they walked from his uncle's rented car into the Airport, Travis remembered something that he'd pushed way to the back of his mind. It came back to the front of his brain like a physical blow to the head and a karate kick to the chest.

Now he remembered. This was the same uncle who'd come to their house the spring before he started kindergarten. He'd taken Chris, their older brother, away. Chris was the child his mother had when she was in high school. This uncle and his wife had kept Chris while his mother was in college, but when she got her job in Texas, she'd taken Chris with her.

The uncle and his wife had been heart broken. When they heard through the family grapevine that Sam Burrell couldn't pay the rent, so they kept getting evicted every other month and that his sister had started using drugs, he came and got Chris.

If it hadn't hurt so bad, it would have been funny how losing Chris had made their Dad start taking care of business-paying the rent-taking it to the rental office himself, making sure the lights stayed on and that there was some food in the house.

Yes, when it came to what had happened with Chris, Travis had used one of the primary survival tactics of children whose very survival depends on their being able to put their deepest hurts into the sea of forgetfulness. No one, especially a child, could live through all the hurts they suffered without the ability to selectively forget.

He'd put the day that Chris had been taken away with the memory of what those white men had done to him and Anthony.

But now the memory of Chris was back in the front of his mind because his uncle stopping Miss Woodlock from adopting them just had to be so he could adopt them like he adopted Chris. It was the only thing that made sense to Travis.

Wanting them for himself, wasn't why his uncle had stopped the adoption. He made that clear as they waited to board the plane.

He said, "I'm taking you boys to your mother. She's moved back to High Point. She's finished rehabilitation. I can honestly say that she looks like herself again. When we get there, you'll be meeting the real Lisa Gregory for the first time in your lives."

The Dallas/Fort Worth International Airport was one of the largest airports in the world. Any other time when Travis was experiencing something new, his eyes were wide open trying to take-in as much as possible. This time he sat listlessly next to Anthony who was still sniffling and saying, "I want Mama Woodlock."

Travis should have been excited. Including the six months they'd spent in and out of Buckner Baptist Home for Children, and the time they'd spent with Miss Woodlock it had been more than two years since they'd seen their mother and their brother Rodney. Their uncle hadn't said anything about their Dad, so Travis assumed that this being reunited didn't include him.

Travis didn't care.

He hadn't cared enough to look around at the street signs and buildings as his uncle drove to the airport. Even though this was his first airplane ride and his Uncle John gave him the window seat, Travis didn't bother to look out the window. It didn't matter where he was or where they were going as long as they were going away from Miss Woodlock.

He just didn't care.

Chapter

13

his was it? Their Uncle John had stopped the adoption, taken them away from Grandma Woodlock and Miss Woodlock and brought them from Dallas, Texas to High Point, North Carolina for this?

When they got off the plane, Uncle John's wife, Chris, their Mom, and Rodney were sitting in the waiting area. Travis had to admit that his Mother looked much better than she'd looked the last time he saw her, but there was nowhere for her to go, but up from where she'd been two years ago.

He'd seen her look that good before and swear-out that this time would be different. She'd claim that this time was it. That this time would be the one in which she finally turned the page-turned away from the drugs. That it would be a new chapter to their story.

It never was.

Travis barely recognized Rodney. He still looked like one of those cherubs you see on jars of baby food but he'd lost most of the roundness.

It was strange. Rodney remembered Anthony and he went right into Anthony's arms when Anthony called him by their nickname for him, Lil Man; but no amount of coaxing would get him to leave Anthony and go to his mother or to Travis.

They stayed with their Uncle John for about six weeks until he got them into public housing. Usually, it took anywhere from six months to a year after being approved to live in public housing to actually get into one. Sometimes, families waited even longer than that to get approved, but their Uncle John had a lot of pull in High Point.

Juanita Hills Housing Projects. The people who built Projects in the United States must have used the same architect because Juanita Hills Housing Projects was almost exactly like Turner Courts in Dallas, Texas. The red brick exteriors made the buildings look like sentinels standing guard to prevent the occupants from moving beyond East Russell Street. It had the same multi-family one and two-story apartment buildings and single-family dwellings. It had a management office, community center, playground facilities and you could get on a bus at the corner of the streets at the front or back end of the buildings. It was Turner Courts all over again.

Uncle John had already had their records sent to Oak Hill Elementary School. Travis and Anthony could walk to school.

Travis rather liked the living quarters in the Projects. During the time when they were being evicted every couple of months, they lived in some pretty bad rat infested, unheated, rundown places. At least in the Projects, water and heat were included in the rent.

It wasn't the fact that they were going back to the projects that had Travis worried. He'd been born into the drug culture of the 1980s and he'd lived up close and personally within that culture most of his life. It wasn't being judgmental for him to instantly label Juanita Hills Housing as part of that culture. He couldn't explain it. But people, especially children, who have lived it never lose that uneasy crappie feeling that comes over them whenever they were in a similar situation or place.

He didn't have to see people on the corner making a quick deal or get a whiff of someone smoking something that he knew wasn't a regular cigarette to know what was going on.

He just knew.

Just like Turner Courts, there were good people like Byron's Mom living in Juanita Hills, but almost everyone there had a brother, a sister, a mother, a father, a niece, a nephew, a daughter, a son, or a grandchild who'd gotten involved in a relationship with what people on the street called the "White Lady."

That White Lady was so jealous and greedy for everything her lovers had or ever hoped to have that she made it impossible for those who were into her to love anybody else. Not their mother. Not their father. Not their brothers or sisters. Not their wife. Nor their Grandmas, Not their children. Not even themselves.

Travis had seen it in the desperation and hopelessness of the mother who had to beg the other women at the bus stop for bus money so she could get to work.

She shamefacedly apologized.

She said, "I was so tired when I got in yesterday. All Miss Lucie's young'uns got the flu and I spent the day cleaning up after them. One after the other throwing up all day. I missed the last bus and had to walk three miles to transfer. When I finally got home, I sat down for just a minute. Just a minute. I fell asleep without hiding my money."

She didn't have to go into the details because every one of the women standing at the bus stop had experienced the same thing. Money missing. Wedding rings that had been taken off just long enough to make the biscuits disappeared into thin air. The gleaning card with the quarters that had been collected for the church's Building Fund and hidden so well that the hiding place had been nearly forgotten turned up missing on the night it was supposed to be presented to the church.

They all knew.

One-woman Travis knew about got put out of the Projects because while she was working a third shift job her husband and a couple of his crackhead friends loaded the refrigerator and stove that belonged to the Housing Authority onto a truck and sold them. They'd set the baby's milk on the table to get sour.

Travis knew that this wasn't a good place for them.

Every time he looked around at their new home, all Travis could do was shake his head in disbelief. They claimed he had a learning disability, but even he had enough sense to know that putting a former crackhead like his Mom in public housing was like putting a dieting fat lady in a house between a bakery and a candy shop. Travis looked at his Mom and figured the odds. He'd give her a month.

It didn't take her but two weeks.

At first, she tried to be slick about it, waiting until the boys were in bed to make her run. Travis knew when she went out and how long it took her to get back.

While he was with Miss Woodlock, Travis began sleeping for long periods of time during the night- sometimes as much as an hour. Once in a while, he'd even slept until three or four-o-clock in the morning. As soon as he was back with his mother, he went back into all-night-full-alert mode. He was back to protecting his brothers.

Of course, his mother managed to keep the fact that she was back to using drugs from Uncle John for a couple of months. Uncle John made the mistake of stopping by to check on her at about the same time on Tuesdays, Fridays, and Sundays. It was amazing how no matter how messed up his mother was a half hour before her brother got there, she'd go in the bathroom with her make-up case and come out looking like Halle Berry. Almost.

She looked pretty good, but Travis figured that a cop shouldn't have been fooled. All the signs were there-the glassy eyes, the nervous hands, the sentence fragments that started nowhere and ended up in between here and there.

Travis thought that his Uncle John just saw what he wanted to see-his baby sister-Little Lisa.

Travis had never known that woman.

Chapter

14

Travis was angry. He wanted to fight the whole world and everyone in it. He hated his new school. When his school records came from Texas, he was placed in a special education class. He hated his teachers too. Deep down, Travis knew that it wasn't the school or the teachers that he hated. He hated that they weren't in Dallas, Texas and he hated that none of the teachers were Miss Woodlock.

He couldn't understand why no one asked him or Anthony whether or not they wanted to stay with Miss Woodlock or go back with their mother. All the foster kids he'd met through the years said that once a foster child was 8 years old, they had some say-so in their placement.

Even though they missed their younger brother Rodney, they stopped worrying about him after Miss Rivers told them a few months after they were in foster care that everyone wanted Rodney because he was such a cute little boy and that he was in what they called prime placement (a home with a foster mother and father).

Travis was sure that both of them would have opted to stay with Miss Woodlock if asked, but no one asked them.

After the first three months, his mother didn't bother to pretend to be straight. Travis felt sure that his Uncle knew what was going on. He stopped coming over to check on her and to make sure that there was food in the house. Because he and Anthony had become accustomed to eating three well planned balanced meals each day, now, being hungry all the time walloped them.

There was no Ma Turner or good neighbor like Byron's Mom to give them regular handouts. The people in Juanita Hills saw Travis and his family as outsiders. Their Uncle John had made a point of driving his patrol car whenever he came by during the day. He seemed to think that the fact that he was a police officer gave his sister and her children an added level of protection.

What it did was set them apart in a negative way. The people in Juanita Hills Housing didn't trust their Mom. For all the people in Juanita Hills Housing knew, she wasn't really out there on drugs. Maybe she was undercover. A couple of people remembered her from high school and the big-time scholarship she'd gotten to go to college to be a chemical engineer. Those people refused to believe that the Lisa Gregory that they knew back in high school had come down that low.

But she had.

They were hungry again.

They were left alone to fend for themselves-again.

One day, everything changed in the blink of the eye. The boys were sitting in their apartment trying to figure out how they could make the half sandwich each of them had saved from their lunch last all weekend until they got back to school on Monday. The door flew open and in walked an elderly woman.

It was more the color of her hair than anything else about her that placed her in the old category. She reminded Travis of Grandma Woodlock except her hair was the whitest hair Travis had ever seen.

"Y'all are going with me. No children with Gregory blood in them are going to be hungry and forgotten as long as I've got breath in my body."

The boys just sat there looking at her.

"Well, come on. I ain't got all day to mess around in this hell hole."

Finally, Travis spoke-up, "Ma'am we're not supposed to go anywhere with strangers."

"Strangers? What you are talking about Boy? Just because you don't know me. Don't make me a stranger. I'm your mother's Aunt Ruth. Your Great Aunt Ruth. I got a house for you to stay in and food for you to eat. That's all y'all need to know. Now, come on here." After making that speech, she turned and walked out the door.

"I don't see any reason not to go," Anthony put-in his two cents worth

"Me neither," Rodney backed him up.

"I guess we should go now because she hasn't looked back. I guess she thinks we're right behind her," Travis said as he looked out the window.

The boys took off running after her and caught up to her just as she was getting into her car.

"What y'all want? I don't carry any change for beggar children. You better back-up off my car," She gave them the mean face when she said this.

"Ma'am, you came and got us and told us to follow you," Travis said looking puzzled.

"Don't be lying boy. I'll be 80 next month. Way too old to be raising children your age. You look like boys anyway. I never did care too much for boy children. Boys don't dress up half as nice as girls."

She put her head down on the steering wheel mumbling to herself, "I'm on my way to. I need to get to.

I'm going to…"

She did this for about five minutes. Then she looked right at Travis and said, "Why are y'all standing there like y'all ain't got a lickin bit of sense. Get in the darn car."

That was the first clue they had that their Aunt Ruth wasn't quite right.

Most of the time she thought they were their mother and her brothers that she and her husband had taken in when their mother, Aunt Ruth's younger sister, died. She even started buying girl clothes for Rodney since he looked the most like their mother.

During the times when she was rational, she was a kind and strong person. She took care of her business and both of the homes that she owned. She was a well-respected member and Missionary in her church and she really cared about people.

When she was rational.

Those rational times became less and less frequent in a very short time. Travis started jumping into her car every time she decided to go somewhere. He wanted to be able to direct her back to the house.

Each trip restored his faith that there must be a God somewhere.

She disregarded stop signs, one-way signs, and stoplights. NO-U-TURNS and speed limit signs were suggestions she cheerfully ignored.

God was with them!

The only sign she never ignored was the stop signal sticking out of the side of a stopped school bus. Not once did she fail to stop. Travis didn't know why that was true. He guessed that it was God too.

Aunt Ruth had a gun.

This was a dangerous possession in the hands of a woman who wasn't always in or near her right mind.

That gun was what finally did her in.

One day she was looking out the window since it was the first of the month and she was expecting her late husband's pension check from being a Sleeping Car Porter. It was sure money. The Brotherhood of Sleeping Car Porters (BSCP) founded in 1925, led by A. Philip Randolph, was the first labor organization led by African Americans to receive a charter in the American Federation of Labor (AFL).

Unlike Welfare checks, the pension check from BSCP was a check widows were proud to receive. It said that their husbands had been "somebody" special. So, the first of every month, Aunt Ruth stood looking out the window until the mailman put the check in her in the mailbox.

That day, she screamed, "That fool is taking my check!"

She grabbed her gun out of the drawer where she kept it and ran outside.

"You better put that back or I'll blow a hole in you big enough to drive a truck through." She demanded while pointing the gun at the man's head.

"Ma'am I was just putting your mail in your box.

I'm leaving now to finish my route," He said as he raised his hands in submission and backed away from the mailbox.

"I said put it back!" she screamed like a banshee.

"Ma'am, I'm going about my job," he said as he continued to back away.

"Like Hell, you're going to leave here with my check," she fired the gun just as Travis pulled her arm making her miss the mailman but sending bits and pieces of mail from his bag flying every-which-way.

"Aunt Ruth, Aunt Ruth it's the mailman," While Travis talked soothingly to her, he wrapped his arms around her pinning both her arms down so that the gun was pointing to the ground.

Someone must have called the police because their Uncle John showed up then. He took the gun from her and folded her in his arms. "Auntie Ruth, it's going to be all right. It's going to be all right."

Sobbing against his shoulder and sounding like her old self, she said, "It's not. It's never going to be all right again. I hate being like this. I hate it. Shoot me. Put me down like you would a horse. Put me out of my misery. End it. Please end it."

Her gut-wrenching anguish over not being the woman she had been was so potent and cut so deep that Travis, his brothers, Uncle John, and the mailman wept with her.

For the second time in his life, John Gregory realized that he was up against something that he could not fix.

Chapter

15

After a little more than three months in High Point, North Carolina, the boys were back to being in foster care. During that time, Travis and Anthony attended almost every elementary school in the High Point School District. They went from staying with an elderly lady named Miss Brown and attending Shady Brook Elementary School to staying with Miss Kerr and going to Johnson Street School. Miss Kerr got sick and had to give-up keeping foster children.

That's when they went to live with Miss Whitaker and her six children and going to Montlieu Elementary School. Their time with Miss Whitaker ended when the Social Worker discovered that the living conditions in her home weren't safe or sanitary.

Their next stop was with Mrs. Jackson and her husband.

Mrs. Jackson reminded Travis a little bit of Miss Woodlock. Not in looks- Miss Jackson was the opposite of Miss Woodlock in everything that had to do with looks. Miss Woodlock was fair skinned- only a shade or so from being light enough to pass for white. Mrs. Jackson was a rich ebony brown. Where Miss Woodlock was tall Mrs. Jackson was short. Mrs. Jackson's husband would tease her sometimes saying she was a half of inch taller than a midget.

Instead of getting angry, Mrs. Jackson would sing Aretha Franklin's R-E-S-P-E-C-T. She'd sing the first verse:

What you want Baby I got it.
What you need
Do you know I got it?
All I'm askin'
Is for a little respect
When you get home

After the first time she sang it, Travis, and Anthony would join in with *"Just a little bit."*

Before she got to the second verse, she, and her husband would always fallout laughing into each other's arms and Travis and Anthony would laugh right along with them.

There were other differences. Miss Woodlock had a curvaceous shapely figure while Mrs. Jackson had the plump somebody's Mama figure.

Mrs. Jackson even talked differently. She didn't speak in that classy college-educated language that Grandma Woodlock, Miss Woodlock, and her brother and sister used all the time. She spoke in the rich Southern tradition of a Black woman who'd never loss or misplaced that connection between herself and her culture.

Travis and Anthony called Miss Jackson the Church Lady. Not because they spent more time in church while they were with her than they had spent while they were with Miss Woodlock, but because she wore a church hat everywhere, she went.

Now, she made it clear that there was a difference between the hats she wore through the week and the ones she wore on Sunday.

She said as she put on one of the hats that she kept in the console table next to the front door, "These here hats come from Kmart or Walmart-stores like that. I never pay more than three to five dollars for these hats. You'll see any and everybody wearing hats like these. But the ones I wear on Sunday come from Thalhimers's, Belk's or Angie's Hats over in Greensboro. You won't ever see nobody around here wearing a hat like any of those hats."

She sounded really proud of her exclusive ownership of her Sunday-go-to-meeting hats.

"Who in the world would want hats like some of her Sunday hats?" Travis thought as he visualized the winter white hat, she'd worn to church last Sunday. That hat had so many multi-colored feathers sticking out of the back of it that it looked like she had a chicken on her head.

Weird hats and all, Mrs. Jackson was a nice lady. She reminded Travis of Ma Turner the way she looked out for everyone and called them her Babies.

Although, she and her husband never had children of their own, their two-story, four-bedroom house on Scientific Street in High Point, North Carolina was one of the favorite places for kids of all ages to hang out.

Some of the kids came for the home cooked meals she served every day. Others came to spend some time in the Den which had been turned into a combination game-room and media-room. That room had the largest TV screen Travis had ever seen outside a movie theater.

Another big difference between living with Miss Woodlock and Grandma Woodlock and Mrs. Jackson was their attitudes about chores and how the boys spent their free time.

Mrs. Jackson worked as a maid for a rich white family. This was during the time that Colored maids were super women. They did it all- they were nannies, cooks, housekeepers, and they even served as waitresses and caterers when the family they worked for had parties.

She was adamant that she didn't need or want the boys helping her keep up her own home. She'd get home from work at 5:30p.m. and have dinner on the table, hot homemade biscuits, and all, by 6:15p.m.

Mrs. Jackson did all the housework and Mr. Jackson did all the yardwork. All she wanted the boys to do was to be children. Her children.

Mr. Jackson was the boy's first role model of manhood. He came to be what they expected of African American men who were in their late fifties or early sixties. He had a high paying management job at a factory in Greenville, South Carolina. He worked third shift, so he was at home every day. Although Mrs. Jackson worked, he made it clear that the money she made was "her money." He paid all the bills.

He felt that Travis and Anthony had been the worst kind of neglected because they'd never been involved in any kind of recreational sports.

He took the boys out for football and basketball. Although Travis found that he really liked both sports, Anthony just put up with it. He felt both sports wasted too much energy and he was trying to save himself and store up body fat like a hibernating bear. He knew hard times would be coming again.

Life with the Jackson's was just too good to be true.

Chapter
16

One of the best things about living with the Jackson's was going to Jamestown Elementary School. Mrs. Jackson insisted that Travis be retested.

She declared, "Those people in Texas must be blind in one eye and can't see out the other one. Something was wrong with them if they couldn't see that my Baby is smart as a whip."

This time, when Travis was tested there no blob of gum and the school psychologist who tested him was a tall skinny man with glasses with lenses so thick that it was impossible to tell what color his eyes were.

He talked to Travis for a while. Asking him questions about his favorite subject in school and about what he liked to do after school and teasing him about whether or not he had a girlfriend.

By the time, the man actually started the test, Travis had decided that he liked him even though his jokes were kind of corny.

As the man went through each section of the test, he made it kind of like a competition. He'd say something like, "The last boy I tested got three out of five right in this section. Let's see if you can beat that.

By playing both football and basketball, Travis discovered that he had a very competitive nature. So, having Travis compete with other imaginary students on a test that really had no right or wrong answers made Travis want to do well.

When the school psychologist wrote up his findings, he pronounced Travis free of any educational deficiencies or learning disabilities.

Next, Mrs. Jackson went to work on getting Anthony out of special education classes. When she demanded to see a current Individual Educational Plan based on his specific learning disability. The guidance counselor discovered that there was no record of Anthony ever being tested for special needs.

Both boys were placed in regular classes.

The boys felt normal both in school and out of school. Both boys knew they were smart out of school- hadn't they taken care of themselves and their little brother for over half a year? It was in school where they were made to feel dumb.

Not at Jamestown Elementary. Not with Mrs. Jackson.

Whenever they brought an art project or a paper with an A or check + on it, Mrs. Jackson put the picture or paper up on the bulletin board in the kitchen and when the bulletin board became too crowded, she put their work in a scrapbook that she kept on the coffee table in the front room.

Every time she had company, she'd show off their work and brag, "My Boys have to be the smartest children in the whole wide world.

That's what she called them, "My Boys." And everything about the way she treated them gave them a sense of belonging.

Because they were growing boys, they outgrew their clothes almost as fast as she bought them. She never fussed about having to buy them new clothes or cut corners by buying them used or inexpensive clothing.

When they went shopping, she always said, "Nothing but the best for My Boys."

Although Mr. Jackson wasn't stingy or anything like that, his idea of what was the best didn't always mash with what the boys thought was the best. Like almost every other boy or young man in 1987, they wanted Air Jordan's.

Mr. Jackson put his foot down. It wasn't the cost. He was old school. He claimed Chuck Taylor All Stars by Converse, the original high -top tennis shoes, were the best tennis shoes money could buy.

He would say with disdain for current shoes and players, "You never heard of Bill Russell or Wilt Chamberlain missing games because of messed up ankles or toes. They all wore Chuck Taylor All Stars back then." The boys didn't complain. There had been times when they'd had to take turns wearing one pair of shoes.

They were happy with the Jacksons. Anthony was slowly beginning to let his guard down. He stopped storing part of his food for hard times when his stash of sandwiches caused an unforgettable stink in the house.

He'd honestly forgotten about the sandwiches. So, when their room started stinking, it never occurred to him that three-month-old tuna and bologna sandwiches could be the problem.

The boys ignored the smell.

They'd smelled worst. Sometimes when they left Rodney's diaper on for two or three days, the brother that finally changed him had to wear a pair of their Mom's panty hose as a mask.

Travis and Anthony didn't think their room was that bad. Yet.

When the stink reached the hallway, Mrs. Jackson sent them to their room three times to find whatever it was that was making her house smell ten times worse than the city dump.

They tried especially hard the last time they went back to their room because dinner was waiting on the table for them. They knew Mrs. Jackson wouldn't say the grace so they could eat until they got the stink out of the house.

That night, they were having porkchops. They loved porkchops the way Mrs. Jackson fried them-juicy on the inside with a crisp delicious golden-brown crust on the outside. They wanted to find that stink!

They searched their room from top to bottom. Under the bed. Behind the dresser. In their dresser drawers. Nothing.

Finally, Mrs. Jackson said, "I'll go find it myself." Since they had never gone hunting with Mr. Jackson and his hunting dogs, Travis and Anthony had no idea how strong the sense of smell could be.

Travis and Anthony had never witnessed anything like it. Mrs. Jackson walked into their bedroom. Took two sniffs and walked straight to the closest. She knelt down and picked up a shoe box.

When she took the top off that box, the smell went up like a Genie leaving a magic lamp after being trapped in there for 300 years.

She screamed for Mr. Jackson, "Lord, Clint! Get this mess out of here!"

Mr. Jackson came and got the box and carried it outside. They all followed him out like a funeral procession.

When her husband got ready to put the box in the garbage can in the backyard, Mrs. Jackson yelled at him,

"Don't put it there. The neighbors will call the police on us thinking we've set off a stink bomb!"

He went to the shed and got his shovel and buried the box under the rose bushes.

When they finally got to the table to eat dinner,

Mrs. Jackson said an extra-long grace.

She blessed the food that was on the table and all the food that God would continue to put on the table in the coming days, weeks, months, and years. She prayed that Her Boy (She opened one eye and looked directly at Anthony) would understand that as long as he was in her house, he wouldn't need to put away food against hard times. She asked the Lord to give Her Boy (She opened both eyes and looked at Anthony) the wisdom to know that even someday when he was grown and gone from her, he'd know what could be put away for a long time and what needed to be eaten right then. She prayed that the demon memories of hunger would let him loose.

She prayed and she prayed for nearly an hour.

Anthony decided right then and there not to save anymore food. He made up his mind that absolutely nothing was worth eating cold porkchops.

Mrs. Jackson thought-up an idea for helping the boys feel secure about never having to be hungry again. She took them to the bank each month and had them split the check that she got as a foster parent into two savings accounts. One account had Travis' name on it and the other one belonged to Anthony. Mrs. Jackson called it their little nest egg. She admonished them to never tell anyone about their money.

While the boys were with the Jacksons, they began to outgrow their twinness- looking less and less alike. Travis remained strong but lanky and slender looking no matter how much he ate, but Anthony grew "thicker" as Mrs. Jackson called it.

Their personalities were completely opposite too. Travis became upbeat and optimistic. Because he played team sports, he couldn't help but be hopeful.

Team sports is always about being hopeful. When you play sports, you hope your hard work at practice will result in a win. You hope your teammate will catch that pass.

You hope your quarterback won't throw an interception. You hope the running back won't get tackled for a loss. You hope the kicker will make the longest kick of his life just when your team needs it the most. No matter how many points behind your team is you hope someone will score the go-ahead points. If you're a true team player, you keep the hope alive up until the final horn sounds.

Anthony on the other hand, never lost his beliefs that every good thing came to an end and that every positive statement had an unspoken "but" at the end.

The Jacksons really cared for them and wanted to keep them forever, but...

Chapter

17

It seemed that Anthony was wrong about the "buts" until the Jacksons decided to adopt Travis and Anthony. At about the same time, the foster family that had Rodney applied to adopt him too.

When the Department of Social Services notified the known relatives of the Burrell Brothers that they were all about to be adopted, the Gregory Family had a big meeting.

Their Uncle John made it clear that now that he and his wife had another son, they could not afford to take on three additional boys.

Uncle John gave a moving speech about how their Aunt Ruth and Uncle Willie had taken him and his younger siblings in after their mother died.

He brought tears to some eyes when he said, "It hadn't been easy for them to take care of three young children, but they knew how important 'family' was. They wanted us to remain together. They wanted us to stay in the family. I'll never forget how much their loving care meant to us."

After several more moving speeches were made about the importance of family, everyone agreed to do their share, but none of the Gregory's had enough room in their home to take-in three little boys.

One of the Gregory cousins was good friends with their father's oldest sister Diane Burrell, so this was how she happened to be there for the Gregory's Family meeting. Since none of the Gregory family members could take all three boys, Diane agreed to take the boys in if the rest of the family would agree to paying $25.00 per household each month. She said she would need at least that much since blood relatives couldn't get payments for being foster parents.

There were 20 households in the Gregory Family. All except three were present for the meeting and Aunt Roxie offered to notify the absent members of their obligation. The way she said it, assured everyone that those three would be brought in line. Everyone knew Aunt Roxie didn't take "no mess."

That's how all three boys ended up staying with their Aunt Diane.

Their Aunt Diane only had one teenage son and the woman knew how to manage money. Based on the commitment that the family made to her finances, she moved out of her two-bedroom apartment and got a three-bedroom house. Even though the grocery bill was much higher than she planned on it being, she made a way for them to have plenty to eat.

The family's plan should have worked. But it didn't because "family" didn't mean as much to some of them as they claimed it meant.

Their aunt did everything one person could do to make it work. Aunt Diane was one hard working lady. She liked being her own boss. She was the first genuine entrepreneur that Travis ever knew. She owned two businesses that she ran herself. One was a dog grooming business.

Like many former Project kids, Travis was too much into human survival to be much of a pet person. It wasn't that he didn't like dogs and cats. It was just that every time he watched people pay big money to have an animal groomed, he remembered waiting in line for coats for himself and his brothers or all the times that he and Anthony had so few clothes they had to take turns wearing the few good pieces.

In his Aunt Diane's other business, she operated a flea market and helped people plan and operate yard sales. It was a business about selling and using what you had to make money. Travis could make sense of that.

His Aunt Diane realized that Travis could not only count money but that he had also watched her during his first month there and taken on her management style. She thought he had potential.

One Saturday, her church was selling Brunswick Stew as a fundraiser and since she wasn't into more than basic cooking, she volunteered her pet grooming business to contribute $10 for each pet she groomed to the cause. She could not be in two places at once, so she left Travis in charge to start setting up the flea market.

She didn't expect him to get very much done. There was always someone who wanted to haggle over the location of the space that they'd been assigned. And, every Saturday, someone didn't show up and there was some jostling if the no-show had a prime location.

Diane hoped that at least a couple of things from the top of the list she'd given Travis were completed by the time she got back.

He'd done it all. He'd assigned the booths to their regulars, people who brought something to sell every week, and assigned new sellers to booth spaces. He'd also collected all the booth rental money and put it in the bank bag with deposit slips. He even got Old Lady Pettaway settled in and grinning like a Cheshire Cat because she'd already made two sales.

Diane was so impressed with his efficiency, that from then on, she allowed Travis to run the Flea Market.

Learning the ins and outs of running that Flea Market was the most he'd learned since kindergarten. It wasn't just how to manage his money; it was learning how to own and manage a business. His own business. It was about being an entrepreneur. His Aunt Diane didn't just pay him to run the market, she made him a partner in the business.

He learned that people would respect him when they felt confident that he knew what he was doing. He was a nine-year-old telling grownups what to do.

It felt good. Real Good.

The first month the boys were with their Aunt Diane eight of the 20 family members sent the whole $25.00. Three sent $15.00 and four sent $10.00. Not all of the ones that came up short had good reasons for it. One claimed that he needed the rest of it to pay his light bill. The others had lame excuses like their girlfriend's mother's sister's cousin needed it to help her pay her rent. Aunt Diane didn't even get excuses from the other five. All of the ones who came up short promised to make it up next month by giving her a little something extra. They never did.

Each month she got less and less but she still had the same bills to pay and the boys seemed to have bottomless stomachs.

When things started getting tight, Travis and Anthony had a heated argument about whether they should tell their Aunt Diane about their bank accounts. Oddly enough, it was

Anthony, Mr. Squeeze-A-Nickle-Until-It Bleeds, who argued that they should tell their Aunt about their little stash. Travis thought it wasn't that bad. Yet. They still had a place to stay, and they were eating regularly. Anthony kept yapping at him about it until Travis finally agreed to tell her.

She cried when they told her.

She said, "I appreciate your willingness to give of what little you have, but I know what you boys have been through. I can't promise that if I accept your money that it will be enough to help me keep you boys with me. Thank you. Thank you" She hugged them both.

Then she finished, "I can't take your money. I just can't."

The next month, she got an eviction notice and her lights were turned off. She went to the Department of Social Services and asked them to find a place where all three boys could be together.

There was no place like that in High Point, North Carolina, or any of the counties right around it.

Chapter

18

The place the Department of Social Services eventually found was in Conover, North Carolina- Sipes Orchard Home.

In 1993, Sipes Orchard Home was still a boys' home. They took in orphan boys of all ages. The same year that the boys got there, Sipe's began admitting preadolescent sisters of its male residents, and in 1995, Sipe's opened the Hazel T. Houston Cottage for girls.

Like most children's homes that opened in the 1940s, Sipes began as a working farm where boys fed chickens, milked cows, and tended crops. By the Time the Burrell Brothers got there, societal changes had caused shifts in the home's programs, staff, and population. Sipes was more than a home for boys who needed a place to stay, it was a place committed to helping the children have better futures.

During the 1970's and 1980's, more boys came who needed therapy for behavioral problems and other traumatic experiences. Students who were majoring in counseling, sociology, and psychology at Lenoir-Rhyne University and

Appalachian State University often did their internships at Sipes.

Although a great deal had changed by the time the Burrell Brothers got there, the boys still did work. In fact, Travis had three jobs. It wasn't that he was forced to work that many jobs, it was because he felt that he needed to work three jobs. The Home gave the boys a clothing voucher each quarter. It was enough to buy the basic minimum.

Travis wanted better than that for himself and his brothers.

The people at the home meant well. They kept the boys neat and clean. He was grateful for that. But the clothes that they could afford to buy with the vouchers had a sameness about them that labeled the boys Sipes Orchard Home Boys.

Travis finished fifth grade at Sipes Orchard Home, but he'd heard that there was a big difference between elementary and middle school. As a young man about to enter middle school, Travis wanted to be more his own person.

He'd learned the hard way that even when people wanted to do the right thing by him and his brothers, other things-other people could get in the way.

When the next bad thing happened to him and his brothers, he'd be ready to take the reins. He'd have enough money to take care of himself and his brothers.

So, he worked in the kitchen washing dishes, cleaning up after meals. Doing whatever was needed. He also did lawn work around the campus and worked in the woodshop. The Sipes Orchard Home made all of their basic furniture-tables, chairs, chest-of-drawers, and desks.

Travis got three checks each week. He saved two of the checks putting the money into his bank account. He spent the other check on clothes and a few extras for himself and his brothers.

Attending Newton, Conover Middle School was the best all-round educational experience of Travis' life. He excelled academically, socially, and athletically. He'd always excelled in math-even when he was in special education classes.

When Travis solved a complex algebra problem as soon as the teacher finished putting it on the chalk board, she called him a math savant.

Travis asked what that meant she said, "It means that in one area-math- you are a genius. You know how to do something without ever being taught to do it."

She added, "I had a student once who could play classical music on the piano, but he couldn't learn how to tie his shoes. His Mom and I finally gave up and she bought him a pair of loafers. At least you have a practical skill that will take you anywhere you want to go in life."

When Travis looked the term up and found out being a savant was defined as a rare mental disorder, he wasn't as excited about being a savant until the teacher explained, "Scientist consider anything that they can't explain a disorder because many of them don't take into consideration what God can do. Count your talent in math as a blessing."

Newton, Conover Middle School, supplied Travis with two things that he'd never had before: friends without responsibilities and not one but two young adult male role models.

Both of his friends played with him on the Red Devil's Football Team. Trey Lutz played a tight end. But it was not his role as a teammate that solidified their friendship.

Trey possessed everything that Travis had always wanted parents who loved and nurtured their children. Trey had older brothers. These brothers teased and taught him how to play different sports. But best of all, Trey didn't need Travis to take care of him.

Travis had never had the opportunity to get to know any white people his age. So, it took him a while to figure out that Trey and his family were different. It didn't seem to matter to them that he was Black or that he was from Sipes. Trey was like a brother from another mother.

Trey was fun to be around. Laughter didn't come easy to Travis. It was the way Trey could laugh at himself and use laughter to make other people feel better that impressed Travis.

One day one of the guys was feeling low because a student-teacher had said his IQ test said he was dull average. Like most people, he associated the word dull with the condition of a knife's edge-not sharp, not able to cut it.

Dumb.

Trey said, "A teacher said the same thing about my cousin Roy Lee, and he graduated at the top of his class. They said the same thing about his brother Ned. Now, Ned was really dumber than a thump. Couldn't count to ten with a cheat sheet. Having teachers saying the same thing about both of them says that all of us are put in the same boat by outsiders. Country means dumb to them."

Travis told them about what teachers said about his friend Byron and how Byron knew the words to thousands of songs. He surprised himself when he shared information about how he had once been labeled and placed in special education. His friends were astonished when they heard this. They all knew how brilliant Travis was in math.

Travis finished sharing confidences saying, "Most of the guys in the class were smarter than the teacher."

At the end of Travis' narrative, all three boys smiled and nodded at one another. Silently deciding that from that point on, they would not allow labels to undermine what they knew about themselves and their ability to learn or to do anything else.

*   *   *

Cameron Pope was Travis' other friend. He played running back and a little defense. Cameron was the only person that Travis would admit to being as good in math as he was. It was funny how different being smart in a rural school was from being smart in High Point.

In Newton Conover Middle School, other students looked up to Cameron not because he was a star athlete but because he was one of the smartest students in the school.

Awards Day, sixth and seventh grade year was basically the Cameron Pope Show.

Cameron's mother had a good job. They weren't rich by any means, but she saw to it that her boys had everything they needed and a good Christian home. Cameron's older brother was a star athlete who was awarded a full scholarship to play football at Lenoir-Rhyne University.

None of the Popes saw his scholarship as a possible way "out." They saw it as a way for him to get a quality education.

Travis wasn't jealous of Cameron because of his family or good grades. It was more of a friendly competition with each one pushing the other one to excel.

Friends had sleep overs. Both Cameron's and Trey's parents welcomed Travis into their homes for weekend sleepovers. When he slept over, both families made him feel at home. Trey's older bothers treated him just like they treated Trey and like most older brothers with younger brothers, it wasn't always playing nice.

That was all right too. Travis agreed that even boys with older brothers needed to learn how to fight back and take care of themselves.

Playing sports nurtured Travis in more ways than he could count. It went beyond his friendships with Trey and Cameron. Middle school sports were different from Pee Wee and Pop Warner teams that stressed having fun learning how to play the game. Middle school was about learning how to win as a team.

The trust factor was a totally new concept for Travis. He'd never before had any reason to trust anyone his age. Once Travis learned that he could trust the other players to do their jobs, he could focus on what he was supposed to do. He became the best defensive back on the team and the best power forward in the league.

The adult male close to his age who served as a role model for Travis was Donald W. Smith the counselor at Sipes. He was in his early twenties. When Travis asked him why he used his full name, he explained that Smiths were a dime a dozen, and it seemed that half the male Smiths were named Donald. He was the one and only Donald W. Smith.

At first, Travis was suspicious of him like he was of all adults in that age bracket. All the other men he knew that were about that age were the type his mother used to bring home, and that didn't say much for any of them.

Donald W. Smith was different. He had graduated from Barber-Scotia College. For a young man like Travis, who came from a neighborhood where finishing high school was as atypical as a ten-year-old earning a doctorate, that achievement was a big deal.

The fact that Donald W. Smith was young enough to listen to the same music that Travis and his peers enjoyed made him almost a Bro. And having a body that was also fit enough to play basketball made him seem like an accomplished big brother.

As one of Sipes' counselors he had regular sessions with Travis. Early on, Travis found himself opening up during those sessions and telling Donald W. Smith things that he'd never told anyone. He told him what the men had done too him and Anthony. He told him how he and a bunch of other guys from Juanita Hills would go to High Point College across the street from the projects and grab as much food as they could carry from a long table near the door.

When Travis laughed about never getting caught, Donald W. Smith said, "You think they didn't know what y'all were doing? They knew. Working in the cafeteria during the off-season was part of my work-study package. What you boys were grabbing was probably food left over from another meal. They just let you think you were stealing it."

Travis didn't have to think about it very long to realize that Donald W. Smith was probably right. It had been too easy.

*   *   *

To Travis, still another good thing about his time in Sipes was that he had a growth spurt that took him to his adult height of 5'9in. At the middle school level this made him tall enough to play power forward on the basketball team and to dominate as a tackle on defense.

Coach Duke became more than a coach. He was a father figure and male role model much like Mr. Brown had been. When Coach talked to the players about turning football skills into real life skills, Travis always felt as though Coach was talking directly to him.

After one game, Coach called Travis into his office.

He began, "My wife and I never had any children of our own. Last night when I was telling her a little about you and your situation. She asked about adoption. I talked to the folks at Sipes and they say it's been more than three years since any family has contacted them about your welfare. So, we could start the adoption process right away. What do you think of that?" He was relieved when Travis smiled, and his eyes sparkled with excitement.

"That would be great Coach. Just wait until I tell Anthony and Rodney. This time we'll be in a real home together." Travis jumped up. Ready to go tell his brothers the good news.

"Wait. Travis we only want to adopt you. My wife doesn't think we can handle all three of you. I'm sorry. I should have made that clear."

"Just me? Not my brothers too? I can't do that. I can't leave them." Travis didn't get into the story about what it felt like when one brother was separated from the others. The hurt and the shame about not being good enough to take out of a hellish life was still too deep.

Travis got up and went to the door, "Thanks anyway Coach, but we're a package deal."

At the end of his eight-grade year, Travis was the first recipient of the Dale Jarrett Award at Newton Conover Middle School, the Sportsmanship Award in Basketball, and the Math Excellence Award.

After a year like that, Travis' actions that summer simply made no sense to anyone who thought they knew him.

Chapter

19

They called him Chaz. He was a big wheel in Bowman Cottage where the high school age boys at Sipes lived. Chaz was going to be a senior in the fall. He was a big wheel mainly because of his size and the fact that he had been out there on the other side of the drug culture. The side that made money. He claimed to know things and he was more than willing to "school" younger guys like Travis.

Almost all the other boys at Sipes had been on the downside-parents using drugs or selling just enough to get themselves their next fix.

Travis, because of his exemplary achievements in eighth grade and his size, was moved up from the middle school cottage, Baumgardner Cottage, to Bowman.

A couple of days after he got there, Travis commented with pride that he'd gotten a five-cent per hour raise on all of his checks. He now made a whopping $40.50 on each of his checks.

Chaz looking over his shoulder made a dismissive sound and said, "Is that all they pay you? Man, you are some kind of pitiful. You work like a slave around here and you're glad to get that chump change."

Thus, began the summer of Travis' discontent.

Chaz kept yapping at him about how Sipes was using him like a prison laborer. Taking advantage of his problem's with his parents to get practically free labor.

Chaz said, "If you are really serious about making some big-time money, you'll run away with me. I got some cousins that have a lock on Hickory. Man, you could make ten times what you make in a week in a couple of hours. I'm out of here in a couple of days. If you want to make some big-time money, you'll come with me."

Travis listened to Chaz. For some inexplicable reason, Travis didn't allow his mind to make the connection between the big money Chaz trumpeted making selling drugs and the derelict life he and his brothers had led because of those same illegal drugs. It seemed only fair to him that it was his turn to reap the harvest instead of the leavings.

Besides, he been the victim of his mother's bad choices. That's the way he saw her drug use. Using drugs becoming a crackhead- was simply a bad choice that people like his mother made. Travis equated drug use with other life choices that people make in much the same way that some people see homosexuality as a choice.

So, he ran away from Sipes with Chaz.

*   *   *

Chaz lived in a part of Hickory, North Carolina called Hickory Hills. It was the epicenter of the drug culture in that small town. People used and made drug deals openly on the streets.

The first week he lived with Chaz and his cousins, they treated him like a younger brother who'd been away in Juvie or foster care.

Near the end of that first week, their attitude began to change. They said they were tired of carrying Travis' dead weight. He had to start earning his keep. They kicked him out on Sunday morning.

Since it was summer, living on the Street wasn't so bad. June days were usually as warm as 84° and never got much cooler than 64°. The Block was alive 24/7.

During the day, Travis hung around on the corner near Knox Store and watched Play Low in action. Play Low was a drug supplier. He was in his early twenties; had a light brown complexion, wore a neat fade haircut and urban gear. He wasn't into a lot of bling, but his watch was a real Rolex and his one chain was at least eighteen carat gold.

Play Low seemed to always be busy. So, Travis was surprised when Play Low looked straight at him one day and said, "Come here, Boy."

Normally, Travis would not have responded to a command that ended with Boy, but he was curious. He hadn't said or done anything to be noticed.

Travis walked over and said, "Sir?"

"Well now, the kid knows how to talk to his elders. Why have you been watching me?" Play Low wasn't bothered all that much by being watched, but he'd noticed that the kid was living on the Street. He'd been there. So, he sympathized with the kid.

"Watching you do what you do. They say you're the best." Travis was just stating fact.

"What they?"

"Chaz. His cousins and brothers."

"They're low-life's. You must be from that Home."

"How do you know that?" Even though he was currently living on the Street, Travis kept himself neat and clean. He knew his clothes were better quality than what most of the guys who lived at the home wore.

"I know because that's what Chaz does. He recruits boys like you to work for them."

"Not me. They put me out."

"That's how it works. They plant the seeds about making big money, then put you out on the street. You get hungry and tired and go back to them. Begging them to take you in. Then they've got you."

"Not me. I'll be my own boss. When I'm ready."

"I almost believe you mean that. Here, take this and get me a soda and a pack of gum," Play Low handed Travis a twenty-dollar-bill.

Travis didn't have to ask him what kind of soda or gum he wanted. He'd been watching him long enough to know that he only drank Cheer Wine˚ sodas and chewed Juicy Fruit˚ Gum. Travis went into Knox Store and came out with the requested items and handed Play Low the correct change.

Play Low was impressed the kid really had been watching him. He counted the change then gave it back to Travis saying, "Keep the change."

This was the beginning of Play Low looking out for Travis the only way he knew how. By schooling him on the ends and outs of dealing drugs. He taught Travis how to cut the drugs to make the most money. How to identify which crackheads would help his business and which ones were too far gone to be of any good to him or anybody else.

By mid-summer Travis was Play Low's most promising pupil. He'd visually researched the market and discovered his niche. Through his talent for staying awake all night he discovered that crackheads that had been using for a long time didn't stay high very long and that if they used dealers who cut the drugs down to less than ¼ their normal potency, their high time was even shorter. Those people needed more drugs during the middle of the night and the predawn hours.

While all of the other dealers were sleeping, Travis was working.

Travis took his school smarts to the street. Since he was only thirteen, he bought a car and hired a driver. He always carried his pager, his cell phone, and his gun. The basic tools of his trade. He banked his money, never having more than two packs of dollar bills on him. Once he established that the account belonged to his uncle who owned a restaurant, the varying constant deposits didn't draw any attention. He hired a pair of crackheads to run his drug business out of two adjoining rooms in the Hickory Motor Lodge and set-up his living quarters in the Ramada Inn across the street.

Travis never lost contact with his brothers. He paid a high school boy back at Sipes to look out for his brothers and to make sure that he knew where to find them when they left campus for a fieldtrip. He'd meet them wherever they went and spend some time with them.

Of all the things Travis felt that summer, fear wasn't one of them. He'd been afraid so many times during his young life. Afraid he wouldn't be able to feed his brothers. Afraid they'd freeze to death when the heat had been turned off. Afraid his father would never come back home. Afraid his mother would come home and bring some more mess.

Yes, he had been afraid, but he'd never been able to show it because his younger brothers would have caught on to his fear and allowed it to pull them further down into the precipice of hopelessness.

In his new life on the street, he was fearless. He held his head high not ashamed of who he was or what he was.

He would have stayed there and probably died out there if two things had not happened on the same day.

Chapter 20

"You're Tee Bee, aren't you?" the boy looking up at Travis was only an inch or two over four feet tall and couldn't have weighed more than 40lbs. sopping wet, but he was trying to look mean and threatening.

"Who wants to know," Travis pulled his jacket back so that the boy could see the gun in his shoulder holster. Tee Bee, his street name was all anyone except Play Low knew.

Still not looking frightened the boy said, "You better stop selling drugs to my Dad. I've got a praying grandma and she said to tell you that she's praying that God will stop you. She believes and I believe that God answers believing prayer."

"I know for a fact that He doesn't," Travis looked down on the boy with a certainty solidified by thirteen years of unanswered prayers. The adoptions that were stopped. The people who were supposed to care but didn't. Travis' eyes looked so desolate and unfeeling that all the boy's bravado melted away like an ice cube on a sidewalk in July.

"Please, Mister Tee Bee. If he doesn't bring some money home this week, we'll be put out again. Mama's big with another baby and Grandma says she can't do no more. Aunt Lizzie and her four kids are already living with Grandma and eating her out of house and home. Please, don't sell him any more drugs."

Travis looked into the boys eyes. He saw all the things he didn't want to see. The heart of a lion in the body of a cub who knew deep down that there was nothing he could do to fix his broken life. He knew what those eyes had seen and felt. Those eyes had looked back at him from the mirror most of his life.

He looked around and noted that several people had moved close enough to listen to the conversation. He couldn't openly show any sign of weakness. He grabbed the boy up by the front of his t-shirt and whispered in his ear. "Who brought you here."

"Grandma. She's waiting in her car at the end of the street."

"Go back and tell her to meet me at the Ramada Inn in thirty minutes. If I give you money here, you'll be robbed before you get to the corner, Travis whispered. Then said louder, "I ain't got no control over what your Dad buys. It's his choice. Get out of my face. Tell your grandma too." Travis shouted as the boy turned and ran down the street. "Where are you going," Play Low asked as Travis turned to walk toward his car and driver.

"To the Inn to rest and watch some TV." Travis replied without turning around.

"You still in business?" Play Low asked mockingly.

"Got to be." Travis said without turning back. Travis realized that Play Low had made note of the change the boy had made in his outlook on their business. It was slight. Probably nobody else picked up on it. But that was what made Play Low so good. He picked up on everything!

Travis raised his hand in the "I'm out" sign and walked over to his car.

"You want to drive some," the driver asked as he moved to get out of the car. Carl was his second driver. He was actually teaching Travis how to drive. When he'd gotten his first car, Travis was convinced that he could drive. After all, he'd been driving tractors around the fields at Sipes since he was ten years old. When he'd wrecked his first car, he'd realized that it wasn't quite the same.

"No. Stay there," Travis said as he got in the back seat.

Travis honestly didn't expect the boy and his grandma to come, but when he walked into the lobby, they were sitting in the breakfast bar area.

"That's him. That's Tee Bee," the boy said.

"What are you talking about? That ain't no drug dealer. That's one of Gracie's boys she was set to adopt," the boy's grandmother stated emphatically. She'd had that scrapbook with his and his brother's work and pictures shoved in her face often enough to know Travis anywhere.

Travis recognized her too.

She and Mrs. Jackson had been best friends since they were little girls. Every three months, they'd meet in Mocksville at the Hill Billy Diner which was roughly halfway between High Point and Hickory. Since neither woman drove, their husbands went too. All of them ate breakfast together then the men would go hunting and the women would catch-up on all the news.

Travis looked so stricken, Mrs. Allen said, "Don't worry about me telling Gracie what you've become. It would break her heart. It would kill her."

"Here," Travis dug into one of the deep pockets of his cargo pants and pulled out his checkbook and started to sign the blank checks.

"I don't want any drug money. I just thought we could ask you to stop. That we could find some way to keep you from selling Perce those drugs. It's killing him and destroying his family."

"It's not drug money. It's the account that Mrs. Jackson set-up for me. It's money from when I was working at Sipes. There's $4,750.72 in the account. You keep it, pay bills, and buy food as long as it lasts. I can't stop your son from buying drugs. He's not one of my clients anyway. I sell late at night. By then, he's run through his money and I don't do 'on time' business."

He finished signing the last check and handed the checkbook to Mrs. Allen.

She took it and left.

Travis went to his room, but he couldn't rest. His Driver wouldn't be back until 10:00p.m. He decided to walk back to the Block. He was so deep in thought that he didn't see the car going in the opposite direction turn into a parking lot and come back out to follow him.

About fifty feet from the corner that led to the Block, the car pulled up beside him. Travis noticed and started walking faster. The car caught up to him.

The driver's side window started to roll down. The way his morning had been going, Travis expected to see a gun pointing at him.

He thought, "This is it. That day." He looked impassively toward the car.

"Travis Corinthian Burrell. Man, what are you doing?"

Travis looked more closely at the man who knew his whole name.

It was a guy who'd grown up at Sipes. His name was Chuck Craft. He'd been a star on the football team when Travis and his brothers got to Sipes. Back then, Chuck was one of the top running backs and safeties in the state. In fact, he was so good that he'd gotten a scholarship to play for Lenoir Rhyne University.

Travis' brothers had told him a few weeks ago that Chuck Craft was back at Sipes this summer running a football camp for the middle school and high school boys.

Travis' first full year at Sipes had been Chuck's senior year in high school. All the football players at Sipes had what they called a lunch buddy. Two or three times a week, the players would come and have lunch with their "buddy." Chuck had been Travis' Buddy.

Chuck took being a lunch buddy a bit further than most of the players. He took Travis under his wing. Teaching him the ends and outs of playing defense in football and power forward in basketball. He didn't lecture Travis. Most of the time he just listened. He'd even come to Travis' eighth-grade graduation.

"Travis get in here." Chuck reached over and opened the front passenger door.

Travis got in the car.

"Man, I couldn't believe it when they told me you'd run away with Chaz and were out here selling drugs. You're better than this. You can do better than this.

Chuck continued reading Travis the riot act, chastising him for his ill spent summer.

And Travis let him do it.

His eyes and ears were open from the moment he looked into that little boys eyes and saw Anthony, Rodney, and every other kid he'd met in foster care. All the truths that he'd selectively dammed up behind a wall of denial came flooding into his consciousness.

All the while he talked, Chuck drove back to Sipes.

"I've been talking to Donald W. Smith and he's worked it out, so you and your brothers are going to a group home in Greensboro. You can't stay here. Those guys would never let you just walk away. All you have to do is not tell anyone back here where you are. Do you understand?"

"Yes." There wasn't anything else Travis could say. He noticed that Chuck hadn't asked if he wanted to go back to where he was staying to get his things. Travis didn't care. He never kept anything that he cared about in the motel. Anything that he couldn't carry on his person, he gave to Anthony to keep.

"Stay here," Chuck said when he stopped his car in front of a small, neat looking clapboard house. This was a part of Conover that Travis had visited often. Trey lived one street over.

Travis watched Chuck knock on the door, and his brothers came out each of them with the two most important items he'd bought- two pieces of luggage. Chuck went in and brought out two more pieces of luggage that Travis recognized as his.

After, Chuck and his brothers stored everything in the truck, his bothers joined him on the backseat.

For the second time in his life Travis was sitting in the backset of a car as though he'd been arrested. Although there was justification for an arrest this time, this time was different. Every other time he and one or both of his brothers were removed from one place and taken to another, there had been dread and there had been fear. He hadn't allowed himself to hope that things would get better since they'd been removed from the Jackson's. He and Anthony were too old for most people to consider adopting them and Rodney wasn't cute anymore. As pitiful as those facts seemed, this time Travis actually felt hopeful.

From the instant he'd gotten into Chuck's car, he was at peace. Although he'd always felt as though he'd been born grown- seeing and knowing about things a kid his age should never have seen or known about.

He now knew that everything that he'd been through had been the making of the Man he was to become.

He could hardly wait to see what was waiting for him in Greensboro, North Carolina.

OTHER BOOKS BY
JO EVANS LYNN

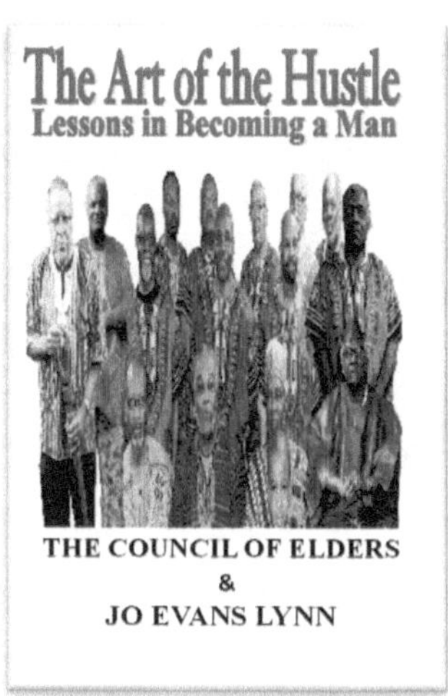

Living to be older than sixty is almost a fine art for Black men in America. The gentlemen of the Council of Elders have mastered the "art of the hustle" in ways that have enriched their lives, their families, and their communities.

The stories related here use the Elders' insights and life experiences to teach what every young man needs to know about work, family (especially about rearing sons), and much more.

This book answers the important questions about becoming a strong, capable Black man:

What is the difference between getting a whipping and being abused?

What is a man's role in his family?

What makes a "village" and why do Black children need to grow up in one?

What is the best way to avoid Baby's Mama Dram*a?* Set in rural South Carolina and urban North Carolina, in the novel **Holding On: A Parable of Faith and Strength**, we watch Sister Fullmore emerge through a very untypical childhood to become a very untypical woman. The book begins on her first day of school, where we see hints of the smart, sassy young woman she becomes.

Her grandma Hester tells her, "Pick your man, don't let a man pick you. That way you know what you're getting."

In all her sixteen years of living, Sister hasn't met one man who tempted her to forget that advice. Then she meets a fine piece of chocolate manhood named Joe Ervin Evans...

"This back is like stepping back and experiencing that time in our lives all over again. Her writing is so real. I loved it!" Toni Jordan

Walk of Faith is about living, growing, and walking in the light. Every poem invites the reader to laugh, cry, sing, and pray with the poet while taking a spiritual journey. Each poem speaks, rather than preaching, to the readers about the universal experiences of all who walk daily in their faith. Even the poem titled "Gentle Sermon" is spiritually and realistically insightful, rather than preachy.

The Promise of Friendship is a moving rendition (but probably autobiographical) of a young girl's life in a Southern inner-city during the early 1950s and 1960s. You will absolutely love Josephine! Her intelligence and quick wit lend the novel an unusual sense of humor that amuses and challenges the reader. The literary style and technique employed enhance the authenticity of the reality of the story. It's absolutely amazing!!! (*JoAnn Eason Williams, Reviewer, Gates County Index*)

All books available at AMAZON.com, or from your local book dealer.

The book is a comprehensive study of the education of African Americans in Greensboro, North Carolina, and Guilford County with primary focus on James Benson Dudley High School. The book is a unique combination of personal narratives from people who lived the history recounted in the book and a well-documented pictorial and factual account of an important time and place in African American history. The book begins with the Antebellum Era and continues through 2020.

"It was an amazing time to understand more about the history of Dudley. Your presentation of your book makes me enjoy my time at Dudley" (Lucimar Ramirez-Rodriquez)

Your book was the closest I've ever come to reading a "living" history about 'us'. Every time I pick it up, it reaffirms what a special place Dudley is. " (Juliette "Judy" Jordan)

"I truly feel that this book should be in every Dudley graduate's personal library." (Brenda Thornhill Holmes)

Book available at AMAZON.com